The Essential Collection for Young Readers

The
Essential Collection
for Young Readers

RUSKIN BOND

RED TURTLE
RUPA

Published in Red Turtle by
Rupa Publications India Pvt. Ltd 2015
7/16, Ansari Road, Daryaganj
New Delhi 110002

Sales centres:
Allahabad Bengaluru Chennai
Hyderabad Jaipur Kathmandu
Kolkata Mumbai

ISBN: 978-81-291-3700-5

First impression 2015

10 9 8 7 6 5 4 3 2 1

The moral right of the author has been asserted.

Printed and bound by Thomson Press India Ltd., Faridabad

Contents

Introduction

To say something about the 'essential Bond', makes me feel as though I am an essential ingredient in a recipe for some exotic dish. I wouldn't mind the exotic dish provided I'm not an ingredient. I'm told that an ancestor of mine fell prey to a group of cannibals on a remote Pacific island, and was served up with breadfruit and shark-fin soup. If that be the case, I'd rather remain 'inessential'.

Occasionally I have to look in a mirror. And what do I see? Purple nose, double chin, double tummy. That's the 'essential' Bond at eighty, I suppose. And in many ways I am a very physical person. I still write by hand. My ball-point or roller-ball pen glides over the surface of the paper without any effort. It has had years of practice. It is the link between my hand and my heart, or between my mind and the letters that form on this writing-pad. Nothing else will do now. I find typing too mechanical. I tried dictating once, but became self-conscious, unable to express myself in 'true sentences'.

Everyone has his or her own way of writing. The 'essential' Bond likes the physical contact with paper.

This volume is a pretty good mix of stories written over a period of sixty years of putting pen to paper. I must have gone through two or three thousand pens during that time. I did not keep the pens, but I kept most of the stories—a few hundred of them, anyway, starting with *The Room on the Roof* when I was just out of school. In those days, most of us in India travelled by train, the air services still being in their infancy, and a number of my early stories took place on trains or at railway stations. You had only to spend an hour on a railway platform to get a story!

After a few years in London and New Delhi, I came to live in the hills, and this is where I have written most of my stories, even those that look back upon my childhood and boyhood in Dehradun and elsewhere. But they are not presented in any particular order. Each story stands on its own. It could have been written anywhere and at any time. Sometimes a young reader comes up to me and asks, 'What happened to that girl on Deoli platform—the girl with the baskets—the one you couldn't forget?'

Well, that story was written over fifty years ago, and it's nice to know that the young reader of today is touched by it. I am now 'old and grey and full of sleep', but that girl on the platform is still there, as young and beautiful and sweet as ever, and I still see her in my dreams. That's the 'essential' Bond—still dreaming...

Ruskin Bond
May 2015

The Room of Many Colours

LAST WEEK I wrote a story, and all the time I was writing it I thought it was a good story; but when it was finished and I had read it through, I found that there was something missing, that it didn't ring true. So I tore it up. I wrote a poem, about an old man sleeping in the sun, and this was true, but it was finished quickly, and once again I was left with the problem of what to write next. And I remembered my father, who taught me to write; and I thought, why not write about my father, and about the trees we planted, and about the people I knew while growing up and about what happened on the way to growing up...

And so, like Alice, I must begin at the beginning, and in the beginning there was this red insect, just like a velvet button, which I found on the front lawn of the bungalow. The grass was still wet with overnight rain.

I placed the insect on the palm of my hand and took it into the house to show my father.

'Look, Dad,' I said, 'I haven't seen an insect like this before. Where has it come from?'

'Where did you find it?' he asked. 'On the grass.'

'It must have come down from the sky,' he said. 'It must have come down with the rain.'

Later he told me how the insect really happened but I preferred his first explanation. It was more fun to have it dropping from the sky.

I was seven at the time, and my father was thirty-seven, but, right from the beginning, he made me feel that I was old enough to talk to him about everything—insects, people, trees, steam engines, King George, comics, crocodiles, the Mahatma, the Viceroy, America, Mozambique and Timbuctoo. We took long walks together, explored old ruins, chased butterflies and waved to passing trains.

My mother had gone away when I was four, and I had very dim memories of her. Most other children had their mothers with them, and I found it a bit strange that mine couldn't stay. Whenever I asked my father why she'd gone, he'd say, 'You'll understand when you grow up.' And if I asked him *where* she'd gone, he'd look troubled and say, 'I really don't know.' This was the only question of mine to which he didn't have an answer.

But I was quite happy living alone with my father; I had never known any other kind of life.

We were sitting on an old wall, looking out to sea at a couple of Arab dhows and a tram steamer, when my father said, 'Would you like to go to sea one day?'

'Where does the sea go?' I asked.

'It goes everywhere.'

'Does it go to the end of the world?'

'It goes right round the world. It's a round world.'

'It can't be.'

'It is. But it's so big, you can't see the roundness. When a fly sits on a watermelon, it can't see right round the melon, can it? The melon must seem quite flat to the fly. Well, in comparison to the world, we're much, much smaller than the tiniest of insects.'

'Have you been around the world?' I asked.

'No, only as far as England. That's where your grandfather was born.'

'And my grandmother?'

'She came to India from Norway when she was quite small. Norway is a cold land, with mountains and snow, and the sea cutting deep into the land. I was there as a boy. It's very beautiful, and the people are good and work hard.'

'I'd like to go there.'

'You will, one day. When you are older, I'll take you to Norway.'

'Is it better than England?'

'It's quite different.'

'Is it better than India?'

'It's quite different.'

'Is India like England?'

'No, it's different.' 'Well, what does "different" mean?'

'It means things are not the same. It means people are different. It means the weather is different. It means tree and birds and insects are different.'

'Are English crocodiles different from Indian crocodiles?'

'They don't have crocodiles in England.' 'Oh, then it must be different.'

'It would be a dull world if it was the same everywhere,' said my father.

He never lost patience with my endless questioning. If he wanted a rest, he would take out his pipe and spend a long time lighting it. If this took very long I'd find something else to do. But sometimes I'd wait patiently until the pipe was drawing, and then return to the attack.

'Will we always be in India?' I asked.

'No, we'll have to go away one day. You see, it's hard to explain, but it isn't really our country.'

'Ayah says it belongs to the king of England, and the jewels in his crown were taken from India, and that when the Indians get their jewels back the king will lose India! But first they have to get the crown from the king, but this is very difficult, she says, because the crown is always on his head. He even sleeps wearing his crown!'

Ayah was my nanny. She loved me deeply, and was always filling my head with strange and wonderful stories.

My father did not comment on Ayah's views. All he said was, 'We'll have to go away some day.'

'How long have we been here?' I asked. 'Two hundred years.' 'No, I mean *us.*'

'Well, you were born in India, so that's seven years for you.' 'Then can't I stay here?' 'Do you want to?'

'I want to go across the sea. But can we take Ayah with us?'

'I don't know, son. Let's walk along the beach.'

We lived in an old palace beside a lake. The palace looked like a ruin from the outside, but the rooms were cool and comfortable.

We lived in one wing, and my father organized a small school in another wing. His pupils were the children of the raja and the raja's relatives. My father had started life in India as a tea planter, but he had been trained as a teacher and the idea of starting a school in a small state facing the Arabian Sea had appealed to him. The pay wasn't much, but we had a palace to live in, the latest 1938-model Hillman to drive about in, and a number of servants. In those days, of course, everyone had servants (although the servants did not have any!). Ayah was our own; but the cook, the bearer, the gardener and the bhisti were all provided by the state.

Sometimes I sat in the schoolroom with the other children (who were all much bigger than me), sometimes I remained in the house with Ayah, sometimes I followed the gardener, Dukhi, about the spacious garden.

Dukhi means 'sad', and though I never could discover if the gardener had anything to feel sad about, the name certainly suited him. He had grown to resemble the drooping weeds that he was always digging up with a tiny spade. I seldom saw him standing up. He always sat on the ground with his knees well up to his chin, and attacked the weeds from this position. He could spend all day on his haunches, moving about the garden simply by shuffling his feet along the grass.

I tried to imitate his posture, sitting down on my heels and putting my knees into my armpits, but could never hold the position for more than five minutes.

Time had no meaning in a large garden, and Dukhi never hurried. Life, for him, was not a matter of one year succeeding another, but of five seasons—winter, spring, hot weather, monsoon and autumn—arriving and departing. His seedbeds had always to be in readiness for the coming season, and he did not look any further than the next monsoon. It was impossible to tell his age. He may have been thirty-six or eighty-six. He was either very young for his years or very old for them.

Dukhi loved bright colours, especially reds and yellows. He liked strongly scented flowers, like jasmine and honeysuckle. He couldn't understand my father's preference for the more delicately perfumed petunias and sweetpeas. But I shared Dukhi's fondness for the common bright orange marigold, which is offered in temples and is used to make garlands and nosegays. When the garden was bare of all colour, the marigold would still be there, gay and flashy, challenging the sun.

Dukhi was very fond of making nosegays, and I liked to watch him at work. A sunflower formed the centrepiece. It was surrounded by roses, marigolds and oleander, fringed with green leaves, and bound together with silver thread. The perfume was overpowering. The nosegays were presented to me or my father on special occasions, that is, on a birthday or to guests of my father's who were considered important.

One day I found Dukhi making a nosegay, and said, 'No one is coming today, Dukhi. It isn't even a birthday.'

'It is a birthday, Chota Sahib,' he said. 'Little Sahib' was the title he had given me. It wasn't much of a title compared to Raja Sahib, Diwan Sahib or Burra Sahib, but it was nice to have a title at the age of seven.

'Oh,' I said. 'And is there a party, too?'

'No party.'

'What's the use of a birthday without a party? What's the use of a birthday without presents?'

'This person doesn't like presents—just flowers.'

'Who is it?' I asked, full of curiosity.

'If you want to find out, you can take these flowers to her. She lives right at the top of that far side of the palace. There are twenty-two steps to climb. Remember that, Chota Sahib, you take twenty-three steps and you will go over the edge and into the lake!'

I started climbing the stairs.

It was a spiral staircase of wrought iron, and it went round and round and up and up, and it made me quite dizzy and tired.

At the top I found myself on a small balcony, which looked out over the lake and another palace, at the crowded city and the distant harbour. I heard a voice, a rather high, musical voice, saying (in English), 'Are you a ghost?' I turned to see who had spoken but found the balcony empty. The voice had come from a dark room.

I turned to the stairway, ready to flee, but the voice said, 'Oh, don't go, there's nothing to be frightened of!'

And so I stood still, peering cautiously into the darkness of the room.

'First, tell me—are you a ghost?'

'I'm a boy,' I said.

'And I'm a girl. We can be friends. I can't come out there, so you had better come in. Come along, I'm not a ghost either—not yet, anyway!'

As there was nothing very frightening about the voice, I stepped into the room. It was dark inside, and, coming in from the glare, it took me some time to make out the tiny, elderly lady seated on a cushioned gilt chair. She wore a red sari, lots of coloured bangles on her wrists, and golden earrings. Her hair was streaked with white, but her skin was still quite smooth and unlined, and she had large and very beautiful eyes.

'You must be Master Bond!' she said. 'Do you know who I am?'

'You're a lady with a birthday,' I said, 'but that's all I know. Dukhi didn't tell me any more.'

'If you promise to keep it secret, I'll tell you who I am. You see, everyone thinks I'm mad. Do you think so too?'

'I don't know.'

'Well, you must tell me if you think so,' she said with a chuckle. Her laugh was the sort of sound made by the gecko, a little wall lizard, coming from deep down in the throat. 'I have a feeling you are a truthful boy. Do you find it very difficult to tell the truth?'

'Sometimes.'

'Sometimes. Of course, there are times when I tell lies—lots of little lies—because they're such fun! But would you call me a liar? I wouldn't, if I were you, but *would* you?'

'Are you a liar?'

'I'm asking you! If I were to tell you that I was a queen—that I *am* a queen—would you believe me?'

I thought deeply about this, and then said, 'I'll try to believe you.'

'Oh, but you *must* believe me. I'm a real queen, I'm a rani! Look, I've got diamonds to prove it!' And she held out her hands, and there was a ring on each finger, the stones glowing and glittering in the dim light. 'Diamonds, rubies, pearls and emeralds! Only a queen can have these!' She was most anxious that I should believe her.

'You must be a queen,' I said.

'Right!' she snapped. 'In that case, would you mind calling me "Your Highness"?'

'Your Highness,' I said.

She smiled. It was a slow, beautiful smile. Her whole face lit up.

'I could love you,' she said. 'But better still, I'll give you something to eat. Do you like chocolates?'

'Yes, Your Highness.'

'Well,' she said, taking a box from the table beside her, 'these have come all the way from England. Take two. Only two, mind, otherwise the box will finish before Thursday, and I don't want that to happen because I won't get any more till Saturday. That's when Captain Mac Whirr's ship gets in, the SS *Lucy*, loaded with boxes and boxes of chocolates!'

'All for you?' I asked in considerable awe.

'Yes, of course. They have to last at least three months. I get them from England. I get only the best chocolates. I like them with pink, crunchy fillings, don't you?'

'Oh, yes!' I exclaimed, full of envy.

'Never mind,' she said. 'I may give you one, now and then— if you're very nice to me! Here you are, help yourself...' She pushed the chocolate box towards me.

I took a silver-wrapped chocolate, and then just as I was

thinking of taking a second, she quickly took the box away.

'No more!' she said. 'They have to last till Saturday.'

'But I took only *one,*' I said with some indignation.

'Did you?' She gave me a sharp look, decided I was telling the truth, and said graciously, 'Well, in that case you can have another.'

Watching the rani carefully, in case she snatched the box away again, I selected a second chocolate, this one with a green wrapper. I don't remember what kind of day it was outside, but I remember the bright green of the chocolate wrapper.

I thought it would be rude to eat the chocolates in front of a queen, so I put them in my pocket and said, 'I'd better go now. Ayah will be looking for me.'

'And when will you be coming to see me again?'

'I don't know,' I said.

'Your Highness.'

'Your Highness.'

'There's something I want you to do for me,' she said, placing one finger on my shoulder and giving me a conspiratorial look. 'Will you do it?'

'What is it, Your Highness?'

'What is it? Why do you ask? A real prince never asks where or why or whatever, he simply does what the princess asks of him. When I was a princess—before I became a queen, that is—I asked a prince to swim across the lake and fetch me a lily growing on the other bank.'

'And did he get it for you?'

'He drowned half way across. Let that be a lesson to you. Never agree to do something without knowing what it is.'

'But I thought you said...'

'Never mind what I *said.* It's what I say that matters!'

'Oh, all right,' I said, fidgeting to be gone. 'What is it you want me to do?'

'Nothing.' Her tiny rosebud lips pouted and she stared sullenly at a picture on the wall. Now that my eyes had grown used to the dim light in the room, I noticed that the walls were hung with portraits of stout rajas and ranis turbaned and bedecked in fine clothes. There were also portraits of Queen Victoria and King George V of England. And, in the centre of all this distinguished company, a large picture of Mickey Mouse.

'I'll do it if it isn't too dangerous,' I said.

'Then listen.' She took my hand and drew me towards her—what a tiny hand she had!—and whispered, 'I want a *red* rose. From the palace garden. But be careful! Don't let Dukhi the gardener catch you. He'll know it's for me. He knows I love roses. And he hates me! I'll tell you why, one day. But if he catches you, he'll do something terrible.'

'To me?'

'No, to himself. That's much worse, isn't it? He'll tie himself into knots, or lie naked on a bed of thorns, or go on a long fast with nothing to eat but fruit, sweets and chicken! So you will be careful, won't you?'

'Oh, but he doesn't hate you,' I cried in protest, remembering the flowers he'd sent for her, and looking around I found that I'd been sitting on them. 'Look, he sent these flowers for your birthday!'

'Well, if he sent them for my birthday, you can take them back,' she snapped. 'But if he sent them for *me*...' and she suddenly softened and looked coy, 'then I might keep them. Thank you, my dear, it was a very sweet thought.' And she leant forward as though to kiss me.

'It's late, I must go!' I said in alarm, and turning on my heels, ran out of the room and down the spiral staircase.

Father hadn't started lunch, or rather tiffin, as we called it then. He usually waited for me if I was late. I don't suppose he enjoyed eating alone.

For tiffin we usually had rice, a mutton curry (koftas or meat balls, with plenty of gravy, was my favourite curry), fried dal and a hot lime or mango pickle. For supper we had English food—a soup, roast pork and fried potatoes, a rich gravy made by my father, and a custard or caramel pudding. My father enjoyed cooking, but it was only in the morning that he found time for it. Breakfast was his own creation. He cooked eggs in a variety of interesting ways, and favoured some Italian recipes which he had collected during a trip to Europe, long before I was born.

In deference to the feelings of our Hindu friends, we did not eat beef; but, apart from mutton and chicken, there was a plentiful supply of other meats—partridge, venison, lobster and even porcupine!

'And where have you been?' asked my father, helping himself to the rice as soon as he saw me come in.

'To the top of the old palace,' I said.

'Did you meet anyone there?'

'Yes, I met a tiny lady who told me she was a rani. She gave me chocolates.'

'As a rule, she doesn't like visitors.'

'Oh, she didn't mind me. But is she really a queen?'

'Well, she's the daughter of a maharaja. That makes her a princess. She never married. There's a story that she fell in love with a commoner, one of the palace servants, and wanted to marry him, but of course they wouldn't allow that. She became very melancholic, and started living all by herself in the old palace. They give her everything she needs, but she doesn't go out or have visitors. Everyone says she's mad.'

'How do they know?' I asked.

'Because she's different from other people, I suppose.'

'Is that being mad?'

'No. Not really, I suppose madness is not seeing things as others see them.'

'Is that very bad?'

'No,' said Father, who for once was finding it very difficult to explain something to me. 'But people who are like that—people whose minds are so different that they don't think, step by step, as we do, whose thoughts jump all over the place—such people are very difficult to live with…'

'Step by step,' I repeated. 'Step by step…'

'You aren't eating,' said my father. 'Hurry up, and you can come with me to school today.'

I always looked forward to attending my father's classes. He did not take me to the schoolroom very often, because he wanted school to be a treat, to begin with, and then, later, the routine wouldn't be so unwelcome.

Sitting there with older children, understanding only half of what they were learning, I felt important and part grown-up. And of course I did learn to read and write, although I first learnt to read upside-down, by means of standing in front of the others' desks and peering across at their books. Later, when I went to school, I had some difficulty in learning to read the right way up; and even today I sometimes read upside-down, for the sake of variety. I don't mean that I read standing on my head; simply that I held the book upside-down.

I had at my command a number of rhymes and jingles, the most interesting of these being 'Solomon Grundy':

Solomon Grundy,
Born on a Monday,
Christened on Tuesday,

Married on Wednesday,
Took ill on Thursday,
Worse on Friday,
Died on Saturday,
Buried on Sunday:
This is the end of
Solomon Grundy.

Was that all that life amounted to, in the end? And were we all Solomon Grundys? These were questions that bothered me at the time. Another puzzling rhyme was the one that went:

Hark, hark,
The dogs do bark,
The beggars are coming to town;
Some in rags,
Some in bags,
And some in velvet gowns.

This rhyme puzzled me for a long time. There were beggars aplenty in the bazaar, and sometimes they came to the house, and some of them did wear rags and bags (and some nothing at all) and the dogs did bark at them, but the beggar in the velvet gown never came our way.

'Who's this beggar in a velvet gown?' I asked my father.

'Not a beggar at all,' he said.

'Then why call him one?'

And I went to Ayah and asked her the same question, 'Who is the beggar in the velvet gown?'

'Jesus Christ,' said Ayah.

Ayah was a fervent Christian and made me say my prayers at night, even when I was very sleepy. She had, I think, Arab and Negro blood in addition to the blood of the Koli fishing community to which her mother had belonged. Her father, a sailor on an Arab dhow, had been a convert to Christianity. Ayah was a large, buxom woman, with heavy hands and feet and a slow, swaying gait that had all the grace and majesty of a royal elephant. Elephants for all their size are nimble creatures; and Ayah, too, was nimble, sensitive and gentle with her big hands. Her face was always sweet and childlike.

Although a Christian, she clung to many of the beliefs of her parents, and loved to tell me stories about mischievous spirits and evil spirits, humans who changed into animals, and snakes who had been princes in their former lives.

There was the story of the snake who married a princess. At first the princess did not wish to marry the snake, whom she had met in a forest, but the snake insisted, saying, 'I'll kill you if you won't marry me,' and of course that settled the question. The snake led his bride away and took her to a great treasure. 'I was a prince in my former life,' he explained. 'This treasure is yours.' And then the snake very gallantly disappeared.

'Snakes,' declared Ayah, 'were very lucky omens if seen early in the morning.'

'But, what if the snake bites the lucky person?' I asked.

'He will be lucky all the same,' said Ayah with a logic that was all her own.

Snakes! There were a number of them living in the big garden, and my father had advised me to avoid the long grass. But I had seen snakes crossing the road (a lucky omen, according to Ayah) and they were never aggressive.

'A snake won't attack you,' said Father, 'provided you leave it alone. Of course, if you step on one it will probably bite.'

'Are all snakes poisonous?'

'Yes, but only a few are poisonous enough to kill a man. Others use their poison on rats and frogs. A good thing, too, otherwise during the rains the house would be taken over by the frogs.'

One afternoon, while Father was at school, Ayah found a snake in the bathtub. It wasn't early morning and so the snake couldn't have been a lucky one. Ayah was frightened and ran into the garden calling for help. Dukhi came running. Ayah ordered me to stay outside while they went after the snake.

And it was while I was alone in the garden—an unusual circumstance, since Dukhi was nearly always there—that I remembered the rani's request. On an impulse, I went to the nearest rose bush and plucked the largest rose, pricking my thumb in the process.

And then, without waiting to see what had happened to the snake (it finally escaped), I started up the steps to the top of the old palace.

When I got to the top, I knocked on the door of the rani's room. Getting no reply, I walked along the balcony until I reached another doorway. There were wooden panels around the door, with elephants, camels and turbaned warriors carved into it. As the door was open, I walked boldly into the room then stood still in astonishment. The room was filled with a strange light.

There were windows going right round the room, and each small windowpane was made of a different coloured glass. The sun that came through one window flung red and green and purple colours on the figure of the little rani who stood there with her face pressed to the glass.

She spoke to me without turning from the window. 'This is my favourite room. I have all the colours here. I can see a different world through each pane of glass. Come, join me!' And she beckoned to me, her small hand fluttering like a delicate butterfly.

I went up to the rani. She was only a little taller than me, and we were able to share the same windowpane.

'See, it's a red world!' she said.

The garden below, the palace and the lake, were all tinted red. I watched the rani's world for a little while and then touched her on the arm and said, 'I have brought you a rose!'

She started away from me, and her eyes looked frightened. She would not look at the rose.

'Oh, why did you bring it?' she cried, wringing her hands. 'He'll be arrested now!'

'Who'll be arrested?'

'The prince, of course!'

'But *I* took it,' I said. 'No one saw me. Ayah and Dukhi were inside the house, catching a snake.'

'Did they catch it?' she asked, forgetting about the rose.

'I don't know. I didn't wait to see!'

'They should follow the snake, instead of catching it. It may lead them to a treasure. All snakes have treasures to guard.'

This seemed to confirm what Ayah had been telling me, and I resolved that I would follow the next snake that I met.

'Don't you like the rose, then?' I asked.

'Did you steal it?'

'Yes.'

'Good. Flowers should always be stolen. They're more fragrant then.'

Because of a man called Hitler, war had been declared in Europe and Britain was fighting Germany.

In my comic papers, the Germans were usually shown as blundering idiots; so I didn't see how Britain could possibly lose the war, nor why it should concern India, nor why it should be necessary for my father to join up. But I remember his showing me a newspaper headline which said:

BOMBS FALL ON BUCKINGHAM PALACE
KING AND QUEEN SAFE

I expect that had something to do with it.

He went to Delhi for an interview with the RAF and I was left in Ayah's charge.

It was a week I remember well, because it was the first time I had been left on my own. That first night I was afraid—afraid of the dark, afraid of the emptiness of the house, afraid of the howling of the jackals outside. The loud ticking of the clock was the only reassuring sound: clocks really made themselves heard in those days! I tried concentrating on the ticking, shutting out other sounds and the menace of the dark, but it wouldn't work. I thought I heard a faint hissing near the bed, and sat up, bathed in perspiration, certain that a snake was in the room. I shouted for Ayah and she came running, switching on all the lights.

'A snake!' I cried. 'There's a snake in the room!'

'Where, baba?'

'I don't know where, but I *heard* it.'

Ayah looked under the bed, and behind the chairs and tables, but there was no snake to be found. She persuaded me that I must have heard the breeze whispering in the mosquito curtains.

But I didn't want to be left alone.

'I'm coming to you,' I said and followed her into her small room near the kitchen.

Ayah slept on a low string cot. The mattress was thin, the blanket worn and patched up; but Ayah's warm and solid body made up for the discomfort of the bed. I snuggled up to her and was soon asleep.

I had almost forgotten the rani in the old palace and was

about to pay her a visit when, to my surprise, I found her in the garden.

I had risen early that morning, and had gone running barefoot over the dew-drenched grass. No one was about, but I startled a flock of parrots and the birds rose screeching from a banyan tree and wheeled away to some other corner of the palace grounds. I was just in time to see a mongoose scurrying across the grass with an egg in its mouth. The mongoose must have been raiding the poultry farm at the palace.

I was trying to locate the mongoose's hideout, and was on all fours in a jungle of tall cosmos plants when I heard the rustle of clothes, and turned to find the rani staring at me.

She didn't ask me what I was doing there, but simply said: 'I don't think he could have gone in there.'

'But I saw him go this way,' I said.

'Nonsense! He doesn't live in this part of the garden. He lives in the roots of the banyan tree.'

'But that's where the snake lives,' I said

'You mean the snake who was a prince. Well, that's whom I'm looking for!'

'A snake who was a prince!' I gaped at the rani.

She made a gesture of impatience with her butterfly hands, and said, 'Tut, you're only a child, you can't *understand*. The prince lives in the roots of the banyan tree, but he comes out early every morning. Have you seen him?'

'No. But I saw a mongoose.'

The rani became frightened. 'Oh dear, is there a mongoose in the garden? He might kill the prince!'

'How can a mongoose kill a prince?' I asked.

'You don't understand, Master Bond. Princes, when they die, are born again as snakes.'

'*All* princes?'

'No, only those who die before they can marry.'

'Did your prince die before he could marry you?'

'Yes. And he returned to this garden in the form of a beautiful snake.'

'Well,' I said, 'I hope it wasn't the snake the water carrier killed last week.'

'He killed a snake!' The rani looked horrified. She was quivering all over. 'It might have been the prince!'

'It was a brown snake,' I said.

'Oh, then it wasn't him.' She looked very relieved. 'Brown snakes are only ministers and people like that. It has to be a green snake to be a prince.'

'I haven't seen any green snakes here.'

'There's one living in the roots of the banyan tree. You won't kill it, will you?'

'Not if it's really a prince.'

'And you won't let others kill it?'

'I'll tell Ayah.'

'Good. You're on my side. But be careful of the gardener. Keep him away from the banyan tree. He's always killing snakes. I don't trust him at all.'

She came nearer and, leaning forward a little, looked into my eyes.

'Blue eyes—I trust them. But don't trust green eyes. And yellow eyes are evil.'

'I've never seen yellow eyes.'

'That's because you're pure,' she said, and turned away and hurried across the lawn as though she had just remembered a very urgent appointment.

The sun was up, slanting through the branches of the banyan tree, and Ayah's voice could be heard calling me for breakfast.

'Dukhi,' I said, when I found him in the garden later that

day, 'Dukhi, don't kill the snake in the banyan tree.'

'A snake in the banyan tree!' he exclaimed, seizing his hose.

'No, no!' I said. 'I haven't seen it. But the rani says there's one. She says it was a prince in its former life, and that we shouldn't kill it.'

'Oh,' said Dukhi, smiling to himself. 'The rani says so. All right, you tell her we won't kill it.'

'Is it true that she was in love with a prince but that he died before she could marry him?'

'Something like that,' said Dukhi. 'It was a long time ago— before I came here.'

'My father says it wasn't a prince, but a commoner. Are you a commoner, Dukhi?'

'A commoner? What's that, Chota Sahib?'

'I'm not sure. Someone very poor, I suppose.'

'Then I must be a commoner,' said Dukhi.

'Were you in love with the rani?' I asked.

Dukhi was so startled that he dropped his hose and lost his balance; the first time I'd seen him lose his poise while squatting on his haunches.

'Don't say such things, Chota Sahib!'

'Why not?'

'You'll get me into trouble.'

'Then it must be true.'

Dukhi threw up his hands in mock despair and started collecting his implements.

'It's true, it's true!' I cried, dancing round him, and then I ran indoors to Ayah and said, 'Ayah, Dukhi was in love with the rani!'

Ayah gave a shriek of laughter, then looked very serious and put her finger against my lips.

'Don't say such things,' she said. 'Dukhi is of a very low

caste. People won't like it if they hear what you say. And besides, the rani told you her prince died and turned into a snake. Well, Dukhi hasn't become a snake as yet, has he?'

True, Dukhi didn't look as though he could be anything but a gardener; but I wasn't satisfied with his denials or with Ayah's attempts to still my tongue. Hadn't Dukhi sent the rani a nosegay?

When my father came home, he looked quite pleased with himself.

'What have you brought for me?' was the first question I asked.

He had brought me some new books, a dartboard and a train set; and in my excitement over examining these gifts, I forgot to ask about the result of his trip.

It was during tiffin that he told me what had happened— and what was going to happen.

'We'll be going away soon,' he said. 'I've joined the Royal Air Force. I'll have to work in Delhi.'

'Oh! Will you be in the war, Dad? Will you fly a plane?'

'No, I'm too old to be flying planes. I'll be forty years old in July. The RAF will be giving me what they call intelligence work—decoding secret messages and things like that and I don't suppose I'll be able to tell you much about it.'

This didn't sound as exciting as flying planes, but it sounded important and rather mysterious.

'Well, I hope it's interesting,' I said. 'Is Delhi a good place to live in?'

'I'm not sure. It will be very hot by the middle of April. And you won't be able to stay with me, Ruskin—not at first, anyway, not until I can get married quarters and then, only if your mother returns... Meanwhile, you'll stay with your grandmother in Dehra.' He must have seen the disappointment in my face, because he quickly added: 'Of course, I'll come to see you often. Dehra isn't far from Delhi—only a night's train journey.'

But I was dismayed. It wasn't that I didn't want to stay with my grandmother, but I had grown so used to sharing my father's life and even watching him at work, that the thought of being separated from him was unbearable.

'Not as bad as going to boarding school,' he said. 'And that's the only alternative.'

'Not boarding school,' I said quickly, 'I'll run away from boarding school.'

'Well, you won't want to run away from your grandmother. She's very fond of you. And if you come with me to Delhi, you'll be alone all day in a stuffy little hut while I'm away at work. Sometimes I may have to go on tour—then what happens?'

'I don't mind being on my own.' And this was true. I had already grown accustomed to having my own room and my own trunk and my own bookshelf and I felt as though I was about to lose these things.

'Will Ayah come too?' I asked.

My father looked thoughtful. 'Would you like that?'

'Ayah must come,' I said firmly. 'Otherwise I'll run away.'

'I'll have to ask her,' said my father.

Ayah, it turned out, was quite ready to come with us. In fact, she was indignant that Father should have considered leaving her behind. She had brought me up since my mother went away, and she wasn't going to hand over charge to any upstart aunt or governess. She was pleased and excited at the prospect of the move, and this helped to raise my spirits.

'What is Dehra like?' I asked my father.

'It's a green place,' he said. 'It lies in a valley in the foothills of the Himalayas, and it's surrounded by forests. There are lots of trees in Dehra.'

'Does Grandmother's house have trees?'

'Yes. There's a big jackfruit tree in the garden. Your grandmother planted it when I was a boy. And there's an old banyan tree, which is good to climb. And there are fruit trees, litchis, mangoes, papayas.'

'Are there any books?'

'Grandmother's books won't interest you. But I'll be bringing you books from Delhi whenever I come to see you.'

I was beginning to look forward to the move. Changing houses had always been fun. Changing towns ought to be fun, too.

A few days before we left, I went to say goodbye to the rani.

'I'm going away,' I said.

'How lovely!' said the rani. 'I wish I could go away!'

'Why don't you?'

'They won't let me. They're afraid to let me out of the palace.'

'What are they afraid of, Your Highness?'

'That I might run away. Run away, far, far away, to the land where the leopards are learning to pray.'

Gosh, I thought, she's really quite crazy... But then she was silent, and started smoking a small hookah.

She drew on the hookah, looked at me, and asked: 'Where is your mother?'

'I haven't one.'

'Everyone has a mother. Did yours die?'

'No. She went away.'

She drew on her hookah again and then said, very sweetly, 'Don't go away...'

'I must,' I said. 'It's because of the war.'

'What war? Is there a war on? You see, no one tells me anything.'

'It's between us and Hitler,' I said.

'And who is Hitler?'

'He's a German.'

'I knew a German once, Dr Schreinherr, he had beautiful hands.'

'Was he an artist?'

'He was a dentist.'

The rani got up from her couch and accompanied me out on to the balcony. When we looked down at the garden, we could see Dukhi weeding a flower bed. Both of us gazed down at him in silence, and I wondered what the rani would say if I asked her if she had ever been in love with the palace gardener. Ayah had told me it would be an insulting question, so I held my peace. But as I walked slowly down the spiral staircase, the rani's voice came after me.

'Thank him,' she said. 'Thank him for the beautiful rose.'

✗

All Creatures Great and Small

INSTEAD OF having brothers and sisters to grow up with in India, I had as my companions an odd assortment of pets, which included a monkey, a tortoise, a python and a Great Indian Hornbill. The person responsible for all this wildlife in the home was my grandfather. As the house was his own, other members of the family could not prevent him from keeping a large variety of pets, though they could certainly voice their objections; and as most of the household consisted of women—my grandmother, visiting aunts and occasional in-laws (my parents were in Burma at the time)—Grandfather and I had to be alert and resourceful in dealing with them. We saw eye to eye on the subject of pets, and whenever Grandmother decided it was time to get rid of a tame white rat or a squirrel, I would conceal them in a hole in the jackfruit tree; but unlike my aunts, she was generally tolerant of Grandfather's hobby, and even took a liking to some of our pets.

Grandfather's house and ménagerie were in Dehra and I remember travelling there in a horse-drawn buggy. There were cars in those days—it was just over twenty years ago—but in the foothills a tonga was just as good, almost as fast, and certainly more dependable when it came to getting across the swift little Tons river.

During the rains, when the river flowed strong and deep, it was impossible to get across except on a hand-operated ropeway; but in the dry months, the horse went splashing through, the carriage wheels churning through clear mountain water. If the horse found the going difficult, we removed our shoes, rolled up our skirts or trousers, and waded across.

When Grandfather first went to stay in Dehra, early in the century, the only way of getting there was by the night mail coach.

Mail ponies, he told me, were difficult animals, always attempting to turn around and get into the coach with the passengers. It was only when the coachman used his whip liberally, and reviled the ponies' ancestors as far back as their third and fourth generations, that the beasts could be persuaded to move. And once they started, there was no stopping them. It was a gallop all the way to the first stage, where the ponies were changed to the accompaniment of a bugle blown by the coachman.

At one stage of the journey, drums were beaten; and if it was night, torches were lit to keep away the wild elephants who, resenting the approach of this clumsy caravan, would sometimes trumpet a challenge and throw the ponies into confusion.

Grandfather disliked dressing up and going out, and was only too glad to send everyone shopping or to the pictures—Harold Lloyd and Eddie Cantor were the favourites at Dehra's small cinema—so that he could be left alone to feed his pets and potter about in the garden. There were a lot of animals to be fed, including, for a time, a pair of Great Danes who had such enormous appetites that we were forced to give them away to a more affluent family.

The Great Danes were gentle creatures, and I would sit astride one of them and go for rides round the garden. In spite of their size, they were very sure-footed and never knocked over people or chairs. A little monkey, like Toto, did much more damage.

Grandfather bought Toto from a tonga owner for the

sum of five rupees. The tonga man used to keep the little red monkey tied to a feeding trough, and Toto looked so out of place there—almost conscious of his own incongruity—that Grandfather immediately decided to add him to our ménagerie.

Toto was really a pretty little monkey. His bright eyes sparkled with mischief beneath deep-set eyebrows, and his teeth, a pearly-white, were often on display in a smile that frightened the life out of elderly Anglo-Indian ladies. His hands were not those of a Tallulah Bankhead (Grandfather's only favourite actress), but were shrivelled and dried-up, as though they had been pickled in the sun for many years. But his fingers were quick and restless; and his tail, while adding to his good looks—Grandfather maintained that a tail would add to anyone's good looks—often performed the service of a third hand. He could use it to hang from a branch; and it was capable of scooping up any delicacy that might be out of reach of his hands.

Grandmother, anticipating an outcry from other relatives, always raised objections when Grandfather brought home some new bird or animal, and so for a while we managed to keep Toto's presence a secret by lodging him in a little closet opening into my bedroom wall. But in a few hours he managed to dispose of Grandmother's ornamental wallpaper and the better part of my school blazer. He was transferred to the stables for a day or two, and then Grandfather had to make a trip to neighbouring Saharanpur to collect his railway pension and, anxious to keep Toto out of trouble, he decided to take the monkey along with him.

Unfortunately, I could not accompany Grandfather on this trip, but he told me about it afterwards.

A black kitbag was provided for Toto. When the strings of the bag were tied, there was no means of escape from within, and the canvas was too strong for Toto to bite his way through.

His initial efforts to get out only had the effect of making the bag roll about on the floor, or occasionally jump in the air—an exhibition that attracted a curious crowd of onlookers on the Dehra railway platform.

Toto remained in the bag as far as Saharanpur, but while Grandfather was producing his ticket at the railway turnstile, Toto managed to get his hands through the aperture where the bag was tied, loosened the strings, and suddenly thrust his head through the opening.

The poor ticket collector was visibly alarmed; but with great presence of mind, and much to the annoyance of Grandfather, he said, 'Sir, you have a dog with you. You'll have to pay for it accordingly.'

In vain did Grandfather take Toto out of the bag to prove that a monkey was not a dog or even a quadruped. The ticket collector, now thoroughly annoyed, insisted on classing Toto as a dog; and three rupees and four annas had to be handed over as his fare. Then Grandfather, out of sheer spite, took out from his pocket a live tortoise that he happened to have with him, and said, 'What must I pay for this, since you charge for all animals?'

The ticket collector retreated a pace or two; then advancing again with caution, he subjected the tortoise to a grave and knowledgeable stare.

'No ticket is necessary, sir,' he finally declared. 'There is no charge for insects.'

When we discovered that Toto's favourite pastime was catching mice, we were able to persuade Grandmother to let us keep him. The unsuspecting mice would emerge from their holes at night to pick up any corn left over by our pony; and to get at it they had to run the gauntlet of Toto's section of the stable. He knew this, and would pretend to be asleep, keeping, however, one eye open. A mouse would make a rush—in vain; Toto, as swift as a cat, would have his paws upon him. Grandmother decided to put his talents to constructive use by tying him up one night in the larder, where a guerrilla band of mice were playing havoc with our food supplies.

Toto was removed from his comfortable bed of straw in the stable, and chained up in the larder, beneath shelves of jam pots and other delicacies. The night was a long and miserable one for Toto, who must have wondered what he had done to deserve such treatment. The mice scampered about the place, while he, most uncat-like, lay curled up in a soup tureen, trying to snatch some sleep. At dawn, the mice returned to their holes; Toto awoke, scratched himself, emerged from the soup tureen, and looked about for something to eat. The jam pots attracted his notice, and it did not take him long to prise open the covers. Grandmother's treasured jams—she had made most of them herself—disappeared in an amazingly short time. I was present when she opened the door to see how many mice Toto had caught. Even the rain god, Indra, could not have looked more terrible when planning a thunderstorm; and the imprecations Grandmother hurled at Toto were surprising coming from someone who had been brought up in the genteel Victorian manner.

The monkey was later reinstated in Grandmother's favour. A great treat for him on cold winter evenings was the large bowl of warm water provided by Grandmother for his bath. He would bathe himself, first of all gingerly testing the temperature of the water with his fingers. Leisurely he would step into the bath, first one foot, then the other, as he had seen me doing, until he was completely sitting down in it. Once comfortable, he would take the soap in his hands or feet, and rub himself all over. When he found the water becoming cold, he would get out and run as quickly as he could to the fire, where his coat soon dried. If anyone laughed at him during this performance, he would look extremely hurt, and refuse to go on with his ablutions.

One day Toto nearly succeeded in boiling himself to death. The large kitchen kettle had been left on the fire to boil for tea; and Toto, finding himself for a few minutes alone with it, decided to take the lid off. On discovering that the water inside was warm, he got into the kettle with the intention of having a bath, and sat down with his head protruding from the opening. This was very pleasant for some time, until the water began to simmer. Toto raised himself a little, but finding it cold outside, sat down again. He continued standing and sitting for some time, not having the courage to face the cold air. Had it not been for the timely arrival of Grandmother, he would have been cooked alive.

If there is a part of the brain especially devoted to mischief, that part must have been largely developed in Toto. He was always tearing things to bits, and whenever one of my aunts came near him, he made every effort to get hold of her dress and tear a hole in it. A variety of aunts frequently came to stay with my grandparents, but during Toto's stay they limited their visits to a day or two, much to Grandfather's relief and Grandmother's annoyance.

Toto, however, took a liking to Grandmother, in spite of the beatings he often received from her. Whenever she allowed him the liberty, he would lie quietly in her lap instead of scrambling all over her as he did on most people.

Toto lived with us over a year, but the following winter, after too much bathing, he caught pneumonia. Grandmother wrapped him in flannel, and Grandfather gave him a diet of chicken soup and Irish stew; but Toto did not recover. He was buried in the garden, under his favourite mango tree.

Perhaps it was just as well that Toto was no longer with us when Grandfather brought home the python, or his demise might have been less conventional. Small monkeys are a favourite delicacy with pythons.

Grandmother was tolerant of most birds and animals, but she drew the line at reptiles. She said they made her blood run cold. Even a handsome, sweet-tempered chameleon had to be given up. Grandfather should have known that there was little chance of his being allowed to keep the python. It was about four feet long, a young one, when Grandfather bought it from a snake charmer for six rupees, impressing the bazaar crowd by slinging it across his shoulders and walking home with it. Grandmother nearly fainted at the sight of the python curled round Grandfather's throat.

'You'll be strangled!' she cried. 'Get rid of it at once!'

'Nonsense,' said Grandfather. 'He's only a young fellow. He'll soon get used to us.'

'Will he, indeed?' said Grandmother. 'But I have no intention of getting used to him. You know quite well that your cousin Mabel is coming to stay with us tomorrow. She'll leave us the minute she knows there's a snake in the house.'

'Well, perhaps we ought to show it to her as soon as she arrives,' said Grandfather, who did not look forward to fussy Aunt Mabel's visits any more than I did.

'You'll do no such thing,' said Grandmother.

'Well, I can't let it loose in the garden,' said Grandfather with an innocent expression. 'It might find its way into the poultry house, and then where would we be?'

'How exasperating you are!' grumbled Grandmother. 'Lock the creature in the bathroom, go back to the bazaar and find the man you bought it from, and get him to come and take it back.'

In my awestruck presence, Grandfather had to take the python into the bathroom, where he placed it in a steep-sided tin tub. Then he hurried off to the bazaar to look for the snake charmer, while Grandmother paced anxiously up and down the veranda. When he returned looking crestfallen, we knew he hadn't been able to find the man.

'You had better take it away yourself,' said Grandmother, in a relentless mood. 'Leave it in the jungle across the riverbed.'

'All right, but let me give it a feed first,' said Grandfather; and producing a plucked chicken, he took it into the bathroom, followed, in single file, by me, Grandmother and a curious cook and gardener.

Grandfather threw open the door and stepped into the bathroom. I peeped round his legs, while the others remained well behind. We couldn't see the python anywhere.

'He's gone,' announced Grandfather. 'He must have felt hungry.'

'I hope he isn't too hungry,' I said.

'We left the window open,' said Grandfather, looking embarrassed.

A careful search was made of the house, the kitchen, the garden, the stable and the poultry shed; but the python couldn't be found anywhere.

'He'll be well away by now,' said Grandfather reassuringly.

'I certainly hope so,' said Grandmother, who was half way between anxiety and relief.

Aunt Mabel arrived next day for a three-week visit, and for a couple of days Grandfather and I were a little apprehensive in case the python made a sudden reappearance; but on the third day, when he didn't show up, we felt confident that he had gone for good.

And then, towards evening, we were startled by a scream

from the garden. Seconds later, Aunt Mabel came flying up the veranda steps, looking as though she had seen a ghost.

'In the guava tree!' she gasped. 'I was reaching for a guava, when I saw it staring at me. The look in its eyes! As though it would devour me—'

'Calm down, my dear,' urged Grandmother, sprinkling her with eau-de-cologne. 'Calm down and tell us what you saw.'

'A snake!' sobbed Aunt Mabel. 'A great boa constrictor. It must have been twenty feet long! In the guava tree. Its eyes were terrible. It looked at me in such a queer way...'

My grandparents looked significantly at each other, and Grandfather said, 'I'll go out and kill it,' and sheepishly taking hold of an umbrella, sallied out into the garden. But when he reached the guava tree, the python had disappeared.

'Aunt Mabel must have frightened it away,' I said.

'Hush,' said Grandfather. 'We mustn't speak of your aunt in that way.' But his eyes were alive with laughter.

After this incident, the python began to make a series of appearances, often in the most unexpected places. Aunt Mabel had another fit of hysterics when she saw him admiring her from under a cushion. She packed her bags, and Grandmother made us intensify the hunt.

Next morning I saw the python curled up on the dressing table, gazing at his reflection in the mirror. I went for Grandfather, but by the time we returned the python had moved elsewhere. A little later he was seen in the garden again. Then he was back on the dressing table, admiring himself in the mirror. Evidently he had become enamoured of his own reflection. Grandfather observed that perhaps the attention he was receiving from everyone had made him a little conceited.

'He's trying to look better for Aunt Mabel,' I said; a remark that I instantly regretted, because Grandmother overheard it, and brought the flat of her broad hand down on my head.

'Well, now we know his weakness,' said Grandfather.

'Are you trying to be funny too?' demanded Grandmother, looking her most threatening.

'I only meant he was becoming very vain,' said Grandfather hastily. 'It should be easier to catch him now.'

He set about preparing a large cage with a mirror at one end. In the cage he left a juicy chicken and various other delicacies, and fitted up the opening with a trapdoor. Aunt Mabel had already left by the time we had this trap ready, but we had to go on with the project because we couldn't have the python prowling about the house indefinitely.

For a few days nothing happened, and then, as I was leaving for school one morning, I saw the python curled up in the cage. He had eaten everything left out for him, and was relaxing in front of the mirror with something resembling a smile on his face—if you can imagine a python smiling... I lowered the trapdoor gently, but the python took no notice; he was in raptures over his handsome reflection. Grandfather and the gardener put the cage in the ponytrap, and made a journey to the other side of the riverbed. They left the cage in the jungle, with the trapdoor open.

'He made no attempt to get out,' said Grandfather later. 'And I didn't have the heart to take the mirror away. It's the first time I've seen a snake fall in love.'

'And the frogs have sung their old song in the mud...' This was Grandfather's favourite quotation from Virgil, and he used it whenever we visited the rainwater pond behind the house where there were quantities of mud and frogs and the occasional water buffalo. Grandfather had once brought a number of frogs into the house. He had put them in a glass jar, left them on a windowsill, and then forgotten all about them. At about four o'clock in the morning the entire household was awakened by a loud and fearful noise, and Grandmother and several nervous relatives gathered in their nightclothes on the veranda. Their timidity changed to fury when they discovered that the ghastly sounds had come from Grandfather's frogs. Seeing the dawn breaking, the frogs had with one accord begun their morning song.

Grandmother wanted to throw the frogs, bottle and all, out of the window; but Grandfather said that if he gave the bottle a good shaking, the frogs would remain quiet. He was obliged to keep awake, in order to shake the bottle whenever the frogs showed any inclination to break into song. Fortunately for all concerned, the next day a servant took the top off the bottle to see what was inside. The sight of several big frogs so startled him that he ran off without replacing the cover; the frogs jumped out and presumably found their way back to the pond.

It became a habit with me to visit the pond on my own, in order to explore its banks and shallows. Taking off my shoes, I would wade into the muddy water up to my knees, to pluck the water lilies that floated on the surface.

One day I found the pond already occupied by several buffaloes. Their keeper, a boy a little older than me, was swimming about in the middle. Instead of climbing out on to the bank, he would pull himself up on the back of one of his buffaloes, stretch his naked brown body out on the animal's glistening wet hide, and start singing to himself.

When he saw me staring at him from across the pond, he smiled, showing gleaming white teeth in a dark, sun-burnished face. He invited me to join him in a swim. I told him I couldn't swim, and he offered to teach me. I hesitated, knowing that Grandmother held strict and old-fashioned views about mixing with village children; but, deciding that Grandfather—

who sometimes smoked a hookah on the sly—would get me out of any trouble that might occur, I took the bold step of accepting the boy's offer. Once taken, the step did not seem so bold.

He dived off the back of his buffalo, and swam across to me. And I, having removed my clothes, followed his instructions until I was floundering about among the water lilies. His name was Ramu, and he promised to give me swimming lessons every afternoon; and so it was during the afternoon—especially summer afternoons when everyone was asleep—that we usually met. Before long I was able to swim across the pond to sit with Ramu astride a contented buffalo, the great beast standing like an island in the middle of a muddy ocean.

Sometimes we would try racing the buffaloes, Ramu and I sitting on different mounts. But they were lazy creatures, and would leave one comfortable spot only to look for another; or, if they were in no mood for games, would roll over on their backs, taking us with them into the mud and green slime of the pond. Emerging in shades of green and khaki, I would slip into the house through the bathroom and bathe under the tap before getting into my clothes.

One afternoon, Ramu and I found a small tortoise in the mud, sitting over a hole in which it had laid several eggs. Ramu kept the eggs for his dinner, and I presented the tortoise to Grandfather. He had a weakness for tortoises, and was pleased with this addition to his ménagerie, giving it a large tub of water all to itself, with an island of rocks in the middle. The tortoise, however, was always getting out of the tub and wandering about the house. As it seemed able to look after itself quite well, we did not interfere. If one of the dogs bothered it too much, it would draw its head and legs into its shell and defy all their attempts at rough play.

Ramu came from a family of bonded labourers, and had

received no schooling. But he was well-versed in folklore, and knew a great deal about birds and animals.

'Many birds are sacred,' said Ramu, as we watched a blue jay swoop down from a peepul tree and carry off a grasshopper. He told me that both the blue jay and the God Shiva were called 'Nilkanth'. Shiva had a blue throat, like the bird, because out of compassion for the human race he had swallowed a deadly poison which was intended to destroy the world. Keeping the poison in his throat, he did not let it go any further.

'Are squirrels sacred?' I asked, seeing one sprint down the trunk of the peepul tree.

'Oh, yes, Lord Krishna loved squirrels,' said Ramu. 'He would take them in his arms and stroke them with his long fingers. That is why they have four dark lines down their backs from head to tail. Krishna was very dark, and the lines are the marks of his fingers.'

Both Ramu and Grandfather were of the opinion that we should be more gentle with birds and animals and should not kill so many of them.

'It is also important that we respect them,' said Grandfather. 'We must acknowledge their rights. Everywhere, birds and animals are finding it more difficult to survive, because we are trying to destroy both them and their forests. They have to keep moving as the trees disappear.'

This was especially true of the forests near Dehra, where the tiger and the pheasant and the spotted deer were beginning to disappear.

Ramu and I spent many long summer afternoons at the pond. I still remember him with affection, though we never saw each other again after I left Dehra. He could not read or write, so we were unable to keep in touch. And neither his people, nor mine, knew of our friendship. The buffaloes and frogs had been our only confidantes. They had accepted us as part of their own world, their muddy but comfortable pond. And when I left Dehra, both they and Ramu must have assumed that I would return again like the birds.

✗

The Four Feathers

OUR SCHOOL dormitory was a very long room with about thirty beds, fifteen on either side of the room. This was good for pillow fights. Class V would take on Class VI (the two senior classes in our Prep school) and there would be plenty of space for leaping, struggling small boys, pillows flying, feathers flying, until there was a cry of 'Here comes Fishy!' or 'Here comes Olly!' and either Mr Fisher, the Headmaster, or Mr Oliver, the Senior Master, would come striding in, cane in hand, to put an end to the general mayhem. Pillow fights were allowed, up to a point; nobody got hurt. But parents sometimes complained if, at the end of the term, a boy came home with a pillow devoid of cotton-wool or feathers.

In that last year at Prep school in Shimla, there were four of us who were close friends—Bimal, whose home was in Bombay; Riaz, who came from Lahore; Bran, who hailed from Vellore; and your narrator, who lived wherever his father (then in the Air Force) was posted.

We called ourselves the 'Four Feathers', the feathers signifying that we were companions in adventure, comrades-in-arms, and knights of the round table. Bimal adopted a peacock's feather as his emblem—he was always a bit showy. Riaz chose a falcon's feather—although we couldn't find one. Bran and I were at first offered crow's or murghi feathers, but we protested vigorously and threatened a walkout. Finally, I settled for a parrot's feather (taken from Mrs Fisher's pet parrot), and Bran found a woodpecker's, which suited him, as he was always knocking things about.

Bimal was all thin legs and arms, so light and frisky that at times he seemed to be walking on air. We called him 'Bambi', after the delicate little deer in the Disney film. Riaz, on the other hand, was a sturdy boy, good at games though not very studious; but always good-natured, always smiling.

Bran was a dark, good-looking boy from the South; he was just a little spoilt—hated being given out in a cricket match and would refuse to leave the crease!—but he was affectionate and a loyal friend. I was the 'scribe'—good at inventing stories in order to get out of scrapes—but hopeless at sums, my highest marks being twenty-two out of one hundred.

On Sunday afternoons, when there were no classes or organized games, we were allowed to roam about on the hillside below the school. The Four Feathers would laze about on the short summer grass, sharing the occasional food parcel from home, reading comics (sometimes a book), and making plans for the long winter holidays. My father, who collected everything from stamps to seashells to butterflies, had given me a butterfly net and urged me to try and catch a rare species which, he said, was found only near Chotta Shimla. He described it as a large purple butterfly with yellow and black borders on its wings. A Purple Emperor, I think it was called. As I wasn't very good at identifying butterflies, I would chase anything that happened to flit across the school grounds, usually ending up with Common Red Admirals, Clouded Yellows, or Cabbage Whites. But that Purple Emperor—that rare specimen being sought by collectors the world over—proved elusive. I would have to seek my fortune in some other line of endeavour.

One day, scrambling about among the rocks, and thorny bushes below the school, I almost fell over a small bundle lying in the shade of a young spruce tree. On taking a closer look,

I discovered that the bundle was really a baby, wrapped up in a tattered old blanket.

'Feathers, feathers!' I called, 'come here and look. A baby's been left here!'

The feathers joined me and we all stared down at the infant, who was fast asleep.

'Who would leave a baby on the hillside?' asked Bimal of no one in particular.

'Someone who doesn't want it,' said Bran.

'And hoped some good people would come along and keep it,' said Riaz.'

'A panther might have come along instead,' I said. 'Can't leave it here.'

'Well, we'll just have to adopt it,' said Bimal.

'We can't adopt a baby,' said Bran.

'Why not?'

'We have to be married.'

'We don't.'

'Not us, you dope. The grown-ups who adopt babies.'

Well, we can't just leave it here for grows-ups to come along,' I said.

'We don't even know if it's a boy or a girl,' said Riaz.

'Makes no difference. A baby's a baby. Let's take it back to school.'

'And keep it in the dormitory?'

'Of course not. Who's going to feed it? Babies need milk. We'll hand it over to Mrs Fisher. She doesn't have a baby.'

'Maybe she doesn't want one. Look, it's beginning to cry. Let's hurry!'

Riaz picked up the wide-awake and crying baby and gave it to Bimal who gave it to Bran who gave it to me. The Four Feathers marched up the hill to school with a very noisy baby.

'Now it's done potty in the blanket,' I complained. 'And some, of it's on my shirt.'

'Never mind,' said Bimal. 'It's in a good cause. You're a Boy Scout, remember? You're supposed to help people in distress.'

The headmaster and his wife were in their drawing room, enjoying their afternoon tea and cakes. We trudged in, and Bimal announced, 'We've got something for Mrs Fisher.'

Mrs Fisher took one look at the bundle in my arms and let out a shriek. 'What have you brought here, Bond?'

'A baby, ma'am. I think it's a girl. Do you want to adopt it?'

Mrs Fisher threw up her arms in consternation, and turned to her husband. 'What are we to do, Frank? These boys are impossible. They've picked up someone's child!'

'We'll have to inform the police,' said Mr Fisher, reaching for the telephone. 'We can't have lost babies in the school.'

Just then there was a commotion outside, and a wild-eyed woman, her clothes dishevelled, entered at the front door accompanied by several menfolk from one of the villages. She ran towards us, crying out, 'My baby, my baby! Mera bachcha! You've stolen my baby!'

'We found it on the hillside,' I stammered. 'That's right,' said Bran. 'Finder's keepers!'

'Quiet, Adams,' said Mr Fisher, holding up his hand for order and addressing the villagers in a friendly manner. 'These boys found the baby alone on the hillside and brought it here before…before…'

'Before the hyenas got it,' I put in.

'Quite right, Bond. And why did you leave your child alone?' he asked the woman.

'I put her down for five minutes so that I could climb the plum tree and collect the plums. When I came down, the baby had gone! But I could hear it crying up on the hill. I called the menfolk and we come looking for it.'

'Well, here's your baby,' I said, thrusting it into her arms. By then I was glad to be rid of it! 'Look after it properly in future.'

'Kidnapper!' she screamed at me.

Mr Fisher succeeded in mollifying the villagers. 'These boys are good Scouts,' he told them. 'It's their business to help people.'

'Scout Law Number Three, sir,' I added. 'To be useful and helpful.'

And then the Headmaster turned the tables on the villagers. 'By the way, those plum trees belong to the school. So do the peaches and apricots. Now I know why they've been disappearing so fast!'

The villagers, a little chastened, went their way.

Mr Fisher reached for his cane. From the way he fondled it, I knew he was itching to use it on our bottoms.

'No, Frank,' said Mrs Fisher, intervening on our behalf. 'It was really very sweet of them to look after that baby. And look at Bond—he's got baby-goo all over his clothes.'

'So he has. Go and take a bath, all of you. And what are you grinning about, Bond?'

'Scout Law Number Eight, sir. A Scout smiles and whistles under all difficulties.'

And so ended the first adventure of the Four Feathers.

∫

Growing up with Trees

DEHRADUN WAS a good place for trees, and Grandfather's house was surrounded by several kinds—peepul, neem, mango, jackfruit and papaya. There was also an ancient banyan tree. I grew up amongst these trees, and some of them planted by Grandfather grew with me.

There were two types of trees that were of special interest to a boy—trees that were good for climbing, and trees that provided fruit.

The jackfruit tree was both these things. The fruit itself—the largest in the world—grew only on the trunk and main branches. I did not care much for the fruit, although cooked as a vegetable it made a good curry. But the tree was large and leafy and easy to climb. It was a very dark tree and if I hid in it, I could not be easily seen from below. In a hole in the tree trunk I kept various banned items—a catapult, some lurid comics, and a large stock of chewing-gum. Perhaps they are still there, because I forgot to collect them when we finally went away.

The banyan tree grew behind the house. Its spreading branches, which hung to the ground and took root again, formed a number of twisting passageways and gave me endless pleasure. The tree was older than the house, older than my grandparents, as old as Dehra. I could hide myself in its branches, behind thick green leaves, and spy on the world below. I could read in it, too, propped up against the bole of the tree, with

Treasure Island or the *Jungle Books* or comics like *Wizard* or *Hotspur* which, unlike the forbidden Superman and others like him, were full of clean-cut schoolboy heroes.

The banyan tree was a world in itself, populated with small beasts and large insects. While the leaves were still pink and tender, they would be visited by the delicate map butterfly, who committed her eggs to their care. The 'honey' on the leaves—an edible smear—also attracted the little striped squirrels, who soon grew used to my presence and became quite bold. Red-headed parakeets swarmed about the tree early in the morning.

But the banyan really came to life during the monsoon, when the branches were thick with scarlet figs. These berries were not fit for human consumption, but the many birds that gathered in the tree—gossipy rosy pastors, quarrelsome mynas, cheerful bulbuls and coppersmiths, and sometimes a raucous bullying crow—feasted on them. And when night fell, and the birds were resting, the dark flying foxes flapped heavily about the tree, chewing and munching as they clambered over the branches.

Among nocturnal visitors to the jackfruit and banyan trees was the Brainfever bird, whose real name is the Hawk-cuckoo. 'Brainfever, brainfever!' it seems to call, and this shrill, nagging cry will keep the soundest of sleepers awake on a hot summer night.

The British called it the Brainfever bird, but there are other names for it. The Mahrattas called it 'Paos-ala' which means 'Rain is coming!' Perhaps Grandfather's interpretation of its call was the best. According to him, when the bird was tuning up for its main concert, it seemed to say: 'Oh dear, oh dear! How very hot it's getting! We feel it...WE FEEL IT...WE FEEL IT!'

Yes, the banyan tree was a noisy place during the rains. If the Brainfever bird made music by night, the crickets and cicadas orchestrated during the day. As musicians, the cicadas were in a class by themselves. All through the hot weather their chorus rang through the garden, while a shower of rain, far from damping their spirits, only roused them to a greater vocal effort.

The tree crickets were a band of willing artistes who commenced their performance at almost any time of the day, but preferably in the evenings. Delicate pale green creatures with transparent green wings, they were hard to find amongst the lush monsoon foliage; but once located, a tap on the leaf or bush on which they sat would put an immediate end to the performance.

At the height of the monsoon, the banyan tree was like an orchestra pit with the musicians constantly turning up. Birds, insects and squirrels expressed their joy at the end of the hot weather and the cool quenching relief of the rains.

A flute in my hands, I would try adding my shrill piping to theirs. But they thought poorly of my musical ability, for whenever I played on the flute, the birds and insects would subside into a pained and puzzled silence.

The Funeral

'I DON'T think he should go,' said Aunt M.

'He's too small,' concurred Aunt B. 'He'll get upset and probably throw a tantrum. And you know Padre Lal doesn't like having children at funerals.'

The boy said nothing. He sat in the darkest corner of the darkened room, his face revealing nothing of what he thought and felt. His father's coffin lay in the next room, the lid fastened forever over the tired, wistful countenance of the man who had meant so much to the boy. Nobody else had mattered—neither uncles nor aunts nor fond grandparents. Least of all the mother who was hundreds of miles away with another husband. He hadn't seen her since he was four—that was just over five years ago—and he did not remember her very well.

The house was full of people—friends, relatives, neighbours. Some had tried to fuss over him but had been discouraged by his silence, the absence of tears. The more understanding of them had kept their distance.

Scattered words of condolence passed back and forth like dragonflies on the wind. 'Such a tragedy!'... 'Only forty'... 'No one realized how serious it was'... 'Devoted to the child'...

It seemed to the boy that everyone who mattered in the hill station was present. And for the first time they had the run of the house for his father had not been a sociable man. Books, music, flowers and his stamp collection had been his main preoccupations, apart from the boy.

A small hearse, drawn by a hill pony, was led in at the gate
and several able-bodied men lifted the coffin and manoeuvred
it into the carriage. The crowd drifted away. The cemetery was
about a mile down the road and those who did not have cars
would have to walk the distance.

The boy stared through a window at the small procession
passing through the gate. He'd been forgotten for the moment—
left in care of the servants, who were the only ones to stay
behind. Outside it was misty. The mist had crept up the valley
and settled like a damp towel on the face of the mountain.
Everyone was wet although it hadn't rained.

The boy waited until everyone had gone and then he left
the room and went out on the veranda. The gardener, who
had been sitting in a bed of nasturtiums, looked up and asked
the boy if he needed anything. But the boy shook his head
and retreated indoors. The gardener, looking aggrieved because
of the damage done to the flower beds by the mourners,
shambled off to his quarters. The sahib's death meant that he
would be out of a job very soon. The house would pass into
other hands. The boy would go to an orphanage. There weren't
many people who kept gardeners these days. In the kitchen,
the cook was busy preparing the only big meal ever served in
the house. All those relatives, and the padre too, would come
back famished, ready for a sombre but nevertheless substantial
meal. He, too, would be out of a job soon; but cooks were
always in demand.

The boy slipped out of the house by a back door and made
his way into the lane through a gap in a thicket of dog roses.
When he reached the main road, he could see the mourners
wending their way round the hill to the cemetery. He followed
at a distance.

It was the same road he had often taken with his father

during their evening walks. The boy knew the name of almost every plant and wildflower that grew on the hillside. These, and various birds and insects, had been described and pointed out to him by his father.

Looking northwards, he could see the higher ranges of the Himalayas and the eternal snows. The graves in the cemetery were so laid out that if their incumbents did happen to rise one day, the first thing they would see would be the glint of the sun on those snow-covered peaks. Possibly the site had been chosen for the view. But to the boy it did not seem as if anyone would be able to thrust aside those massive tombstones and rise from their graves to enjoy the view. Their rest seemed as eternal as the snows. It would take an earthquake to burst those stones asunder and thrust the coffins up from the earth. The boy wondered why people hadn't made it easier for the dead to rise. They were so securely entombed that it appeared as though no one really wanted them to get out.

'God has need of your father...' With those words a well-meaning missionary had tried to console him.

And had God, in the same way, laid claim to the thousands of men, women and children who had been put to rest here in these neat and serried rows? What could he have wanted them for? Of what use are we to God when we are dead, wondered the boy.

The cemetery gate stood open but the boy leant against the old stone wall and stared down at the mourners as they shuffled about with the unease of a batsman about to face a very fast bowler. Only this bowler was invisible and would come up stealthily and from behind.

Padre Lal's voice droned on through the funeral service and then the coffin was lowered—down, deep down. The boy was surprised at how far down it seemed to go! Was that other, better world down in the depths of the earth? How could anyone, even a Samson, push his way back to the surface again? Superman did it in comics but his father was a gentle soul who wouldn't fight too hard against the earth and the grass and the roots of tiny trees. Or perhaps he'd grow into a tree and escape that way! 'If ever I'm put away like this,' thought the boy, 'I'll get into the root of a plant and then I'll become a flower and then maybe a bird will come and carry my seed away… I'll get out somehow!'

A few more words from the padre and then some of those present threw handfuls of earth over the coffin before moving away.

Slowly, in twos and threes, the mourners departed. The mist swallowed them up. They did not see the boy behind the wall. They were getting hungry.

He stood there until they had all gone. Then he noticed that the gardeners or caretakers were filling in the grave. He did not know whether to go forward or not. He was a little afraid. And it was too late now. The grave was almost covered.

He turned and walked away from the cemetery. The road stretched ahead of him, empty, swathed in mist. He was alone. What had his father said to him once? 'The strongest man in the world is he who stands alone.'

Well, he was alone, but at the moment he did not feel very strong.

For a moment he thought his father was beside him, that they were together on one of their long walks. Instinctively he put out his hand, expecting his father's warm, comforting touch. But there was nothing there, nothing, no one…

He clenched his fists and pushed them deep down into his pockets. He lowered his head so that no one would see his tears. There were people in the mist but he did not want to go near them for they had put his father away.

'He'll find a way out,' the boy said fiercely to himself. 'He'll get out somehow!'

Coming Home to Dehra

THE FAINT queasiness I always feel towards the end of a journey probably has its origin in that first homecoming after my father's death.

It was the winter of 1944—yes, a long time ago—and the train was running through the thick sal forests near Dehra, bringing me at every click of the rails nearer to the mother I hadn't seen for four years and the stepfather I had seen just once or twice before my parents were divorced.

I was eleven and I was coming home to Dehra.

Three years earlier, after the separation, I had gone to live with my father. We were very happy together. He was serving in the RAF, at New Delhi, and we lived in a large tent somewhere near Humayun's Tomb. The area is now a very busy part of urban Delhi, but in those days it was still a wilderness of scrub jungle where black buck and nilgai roamed freely. We took long walks together, exploring the ruins of old tombs and forts; went to the pictures (George Formby comedies were special favourites of mine); collected stamps; bought books (my father had taught me to read and write before I started going to school); and made plans for going to England when the war was over.

Six months of bliss, even though it was summer and there weren't any fans, only a thick khus reed curtain which had to be splashed with water every hour by a bhisti who did the rounds of similar tents with his goat-skin water bag. I remember the tender refreshing fragrance of the khus, and also the smell of damp earth outside, where the water had spilt.

A happy time. But it had to end. My father's periodic bouts of malarial fever resulted in his having to enter hospital for a week. The bhisti's small son came to stay with me at night, and during the day I took my meals with an Anglo-Indian family across the road.

I would have been quite happy to continue with this arrangement whenever my father was absent, but someone at air headquarters must have advised him to put me in a boarding school.

Reluctantly he came to the decision that this would be the best thing—'until the war is over'—and in the June of 1943 he took me to Shimla, where I was incarcerated in a preparatory school for boys.

This is not the story of my life at boarding school. It might easily have been a public school in England; it did in fact pride itself on being the 'Eton of the East'. The traditions— such as ragging and flogging, compulsory games and chapel attendance, prefects larger than life, and honour boards for everything from school captaincy to choir membership—had all apparently been borrowed from *Tom Brown's Schooldays*.

My father wrote to me regularly, and his letters were the things I looked forward to more than anything else. I went to him for the winter holidays, and the following summer he came to Shimla during my mid-term break and took me out for the duration of the holidays. We stayed in a hotel called Craig-Dhu, on a spur north of Jacko Hill. It was an idyllic week; long walks; stories about phantom rickshaws; ice creams in the sun; browsings in bookshops; more plans: 'We will go to England next year.'

School seemed a stupid and heartless place after my father had gone away. He had been transferred to Calcutta and he wasn't keeping well there. Malaria again. And then jaundice. But his last letter sounded quite cheerful. He'd been selling part of his valuable stamp collection so as to have enough money for the fares to England.

One day my class teacher sent for me.

'I want to talk to you, Bond,' he said. 'Let's go for a walk.'

I knew immediately that something was wrong.

We took the path that went through the deodar forest, past Council Rock where scout meetings were held. As soon as my unfortunate teacher (no doubt cursing the headmaster for having given him this unpleasant task) started on the theme of 'God wanting your father in a higher and better place,' as though there could be any better place than Jacko Hill in mid-summer, I knew my father was dead, and burst into tears.

They let me stay in the school hospital for a few days until I felt better. The headmaster visited me there and took away the pile of my father's letters that I'd kept beside me.

'Your father's letters. You might lose them. Why not leave them with me? Then at the end of the year, before you go home, you can come and collect them.'

Unwillingly I gave him the letters. He told me he'd heard from my mother that I would be going home to her at the end of the year. He seemed surprised that I evinced no interest in this prospect.

At the end of the year, the day before school closed, I went to the headmaster's office and asked for my letters.

'What letters?' he said. His desk was piled with papers and correspondence, and he was irritated by my interruption.

'My father's letters,' I explained. 'I gave them to you to keep for me, sir—when he died…'

'Letters. Are you sure you gave them to me?'

He grew more irritated. 'You must be mistaken, Bond. Why

should I want to keep your father's letters?'

'I don't know, sir. You said I could collect them before going home.'

'Look, I don't remember any letters and I'm very busy just now, so run along. I'm sure you're mistaken, but if I find your letters, I'll send them to you.'

I don't suppose he meant to be unkind, but he was the first man who aroused in me feelings of hate...

As the train drew into Dehra, I looked out of the window to see if there was anyone on the platform waiting to receive me. The station was crowded enough, as most railway stations are in India, with overloaded travellers, shouting coolies, stray dogs, stray stationmasters... Pandemonium broke loose as the train came to a halt and people debauched from the carriages. I was thrust on the platform with my tin trunk and small attaché case. I sat on the trunk and waited for someone to find me.

Slowly the crowd melted away. I was left with one elderly coolie who was too feeble to carry heavy luggage and had decided that my trunk was just the right size and weight for his head and shoulders. I waited another ten minutes, but no representative of my mother or stepfather appeared. I permitted the coolie to lead me out of the station to the tonga stand.

Those were the days when everyone, including high-ranking officials, went about in tongas. Dehra had just one taxi. I was quite happy sitting beside a rather smelly, paan-spitting tonga driver, while his weary, underfed pony clip-clopped along the quiet tree-lined roads.

Dehra was always a good place for trees. The valley soil is very fertile, the rainfall fairly heavy; almost everything grows there, if given the chance. The roads were lined with neem and mango trees, eucalyptus, Persian lilac, jacaranda, amaltas (laburnum) and many others. In the gardens of the bungalows were mangoes, litchis and guavas; sometimes jackfruit and papaya. I did not notice all these trees at once; I came to know them as time passed.

The tonga first took me to my grandmother's house. I was under the impression that my mother still lived there.

A lovely, comfortable bungalow that spread itself about the grounds in an easy going, old-fashioned way. There was even smoke coming from the chimneys, reminding me of the smoke from my grandfather's pipe. When I was eight, I had spent several months there with my grandparents. In retrospect it had been an idyllic interlude. But Grandfather was dead. Grandmother lived alone.

White-haired, but still broad in the face and even broader behind, she was astonished to see me getting down from the tonga.

'Didn't anyone meet you at the station?' she asked.

I shook my head. Grandmother said: 'Your mother doesn't live here any more. You can come in and wait, but she may be worried about you, so I'd better take you to her place. Come on, help me up into the tonga... I might have known it would be a white horse. It always makes me nervous sitting in a tonga behind a white horse.'

'Why, Granny?'

'I don't know, I suppose white horses are nervous, too. Anyway, they are always trying to topple me out. Not so fast, driver!' she called out, as the tonga man cracked his whip and the pony changed from a slow shuffle to a brisk trot.

It took us about twenty-five minutes to reach my stepfather's house which was in the Dalanwala area, not far from the dry bed of the seasonal Rispana river. My grandmother, seeing that I was in need of moral support, got down with me, while the tonga driver carried my bedding roll and tin trunk on to the veranda.

The front door was bolted from inside. We had to knock on it repeatedly and call out before it was opened by a servant who did not look pleased at being disturbed. When he saw my grandmother he gave her a deferential salaam, then gazed at me with open curiosity.

'Where's the memsahib?' asked Grandmother.

'Out,' said the servant.

'I can see that but where have they gone?'

'They went yesterday to Motichur, for shikar. They will be back this evening.'

Grandmother looked upset, but motioned to the servant to bring in my things. 'Weren't they expecting the boy?' she asked. 'Yes,' he said looking at me again. 'But they said he would be arriving tomorrow.'

'They'd forgotten the date,' said Grandmother in a huff. 'Anyway, you can unpack and have a wash and change your clothes.'

Turning to the servant, she asked, 'Is there any lunch?'

'I will make lunch,' he said. He was staring at me again, and I felt uneasy with his eyes on me. He was tall and swarthy, with oily, jet-back hair and a thick moustache. A heavy scar ran down his left cheek, giving him a rather sinister appearance. He wore a torn shirt and dirty pyjamas. His broad, heavy feet were wet. They, left marks on the uncarpeted floor.

A baby was crying in the next room, and presently a woman (who turned out to be the cook's wife) appeared in the doorway, jogging the child in her arms.

'They've left the baby behind, too,' said Grandmother, becoming more and more irate. 'He is your young brother. Only six months old.' I hadn't been told anything about a younger brother. The discovery that I had one came as something of a shock. I wasn't prepared for a baby brother, least of all a baby half-brother. I examined the child without much enthusiasm. He looked healthy enough and he cried with gusto.

'He's a beautiful baby,' said Grandmother. 'Well, I've got work to do. The servants will look after you. You can come and see me in a day or two. You've grown since I last saw you. And you're getting pimples.'

This reference to my appearance did not displease me as Grandmother never indulged in praise. For her to have observed my pimples indicated that she was fond of me.

The tonga driver was waiting for her. 'I suppose I'll have to use the same tonga,' she said. 'Whenever I need a tonga, they disappear, except for the ones with white ponies. When your mother gets back, tell her I want to see her. Shikar, indeed. An infant to look after, and they've gone shooting.'

Grandmother settled herself in the tonga, nodded in response to the cook's salaam, and took a tight grip of the armrests of her seat. The driver flourished his whip and the pony set off at the same listless, unhurried trot, while my grandmother, feeling quite certain that she was going to be hurtled to her doom by a wild white pony, set her teeth and clung tenaciously to the tonga seat. I was sorry to see her go.

My mother and stepfather returned in the evening from their hunting trip with a pheasant which was duly handed over to the cook, whose name was Mangal Singh. My mother gave me a perfunctory kiss. I think she was pleased to see me, but I was accustomed to a more intimate caress from my father, and the strange reception I had received made me realize the extent of my loss. Boarding school life had been routine. Going home was something that I had always looked forward to. But going home had meant my father, and now he had vanished and I was left quite desolate.

I suppose if one is present when a loved one dies, or sees

him dead and laid out and later buried, one is convinced of the finality of the thing and finds it easier to adapt to the changed circumstances. But when you hear of a death, a father's death, and have only the faintest idea of the manner of his dying, it is rather a lot for the imagination to cope with—especially when the imagination is a small boy's. There being no tangible evidence of my father's death, it was, for me, not a death but a vanishing. And although this enabled me to remember him as a living, smiling, breathing person, it meant that I was not wholly reconciled to his death, and subconsciously expected him to turn up (as he often did, when I most needed him) and deliver me from any unpleasant situation.

My stepfather barely noticed me. The first thing he did on coming into the house was to pour himself a whisky and soda. My mother, after inspecting the baby, did likewise. I was left to unpack and settle in my room.

I was fortunate in having my own room. I was as desirous of my own privacy as much as my mother and stepfather were desirous of theirs. My stepfather, a local businessman, was ready to put up with me provided I did not get in the way. And, in a different way, I was ready to put up with him, provided he left me alone. I was even willing that my mother should leave me alone. There was a big window to my room, and I opened it to the evening breeze, and gazed out on to the garden, a rather unkempt place where marigolds and a sort of wild blue everlasting grew rampant among the litchi trees.

✗

Our Great Escape

I<small>T HAD</small> been a lonely winter for a fourteen-year-old. I had spent the first few weeks of the vacation with my mother and stepfather in Dehra. Then they left for Delhi, and I was pretty much on my own. Of course, the servants were there to take care of my needs, but there was no one to keep me company. I would wander off in the mornings, taking some path up the hills, come back home for lunch, read a bit and then stroll off again till it was time for dinner. Sometimes I walked up to my grandparents' house, but it seemed so different now, with people I didn't know occupying the house.

The three-month winter break over, I was almost eager to return to my boarding school in Shimla.

It wasn't as though I had many friends at school. I needed a friend but it was not easy to find one among a horde of rowdy, pea-shooting eighth formers, who carved their names on desks and stuck chewing gum on the class teacher's chair. Had I grown up with other children, I might have developed a taste for schoolboy anarchy; but in sharing my father's loneliness after his separation from my mother, and in being bereft of any close family ties, I had turned into a premature adult.

After a month in the eighth form, I began to notice a new boy, Omar, and then only because he was a quiet, almost taciturn person who took no part in the form's feverish attempt to imitate the Marx Brothers at the circus. He showed no resentment at the prevailing anarchy, nor did he make a move to participate in it. Once he caught me looking at him, and he smiled ruefully, tolerantly. Did I sense another adult in the class? Someone who was a little older than his years?

Even before we began talking to each other, Omar and I developed an understanding of sorts, and we'd nod almost respectfully to each other when we met in the classroom corridors or the environs of the dining hall or the dormitory. We were not in the same house. The house system practised its own form of apartheid, whereby a member of one house was not expected to fraternize with someone belonging to another. Those public schools certainly knew how to clamp you into compartments. However, these barriers vanished when Omar and I found ourselves selected for the School Colts' hockey team, Omar as a full-back, I as the goalkeeper.

The taciturn Omar now spoke to me occasionally, and we combined well on the field of play. A good understanding is needed between a goalkeeper and a full-back. We were on the same wavelength. I anticipated his moves, he was familiar with mine. Years later, when I read Conrad's *The Secret Sharer*, I thought of Omar.

It wasn't until we were away from the confines of school, classroom and dining hall that our friendship flourished. The hockey team travelled to Sanawar on the next mountain range, where we were to play a couple of matches against our old rivals, the Lawrence Royal Military School. This had been my father's old school, so I was keen to explore its grounds and peep into its classrooms.

Omar and I were thrown together a good deal during the visit to Sanawar, and in our more leisurely moments, strolling undisturbed around a school where we were guests and not pupils, we exchanged life histories and other confidences. Omar, too, had lost his father—had I sensed that before?—shot in some tribal encounter on the Frontier, for he hailed from the lawless lands beyond Peshawar. A wealthy uncle was seeing to Omar's education.

We wandered into the school chapel, and there I found my father's name—A.A. Bond—on the school's roll of honour board: old boys who had lost their lives while serving during the two World Wars.

'What did his initials stand for?' asked Omar.

'Aubrey Alexander.'

'Unusual names, like yours. Why did your parents call you Rusty?'

'I am not sure.' I told him about the book I was writing. It was my first one and was called *Nine Months* (the length of the school term, not a pregnancy), and it described some of the happenings at school and lampooned a few of our teachers. I had filled three slim exercise books with this premature literary project, and I allowed Omar to go through them. He must have been my first reader and critic.

'They're very interesting,' he said, 'but you'll get into trouble if someone finds them, especially Mr Fisher.'

I have to admit it wasn't great literature. I was better at hockey and football. I made some spectacular saves, and we won our matches against Sanawar. When we returned to Shimla, we were school heroes for a couple of days and lost some of our reticence; we were even a little more forthcoming with other boys. And then Mr Fisher, my housemaster, discovered my literary opus, *Nine Months*, under my mattress, and took it away and read it (as he told me later) from cover to cover. Corporal punishment then being in vogue, I was given six of the best with a springy Malacca cane, and my manuscript was torn up and deposited in Mr Fisher's wastepaper basket. All I had to show for my efforts were some purple welts on my bottom.

These were proudly displayed to all who were interested, and I was a hero for another two days.

'Will you go away too when the British leave India?' Omar asked me one day.

'I don't think so,' I said. 'I don't have anyone to go back to in England, and my guardian, Mr Harrison, too seems to have no intention of going back.'

'Everyone is saying that our leaders and the British are going to divide the country. Shimla will be in India, Peshawar in Pakistan!'

'Oh, it won't happen,' I said glibly. 'How can they cut up such a big country?' But even as we chatted about the possibility, Nehru, Jinnah and Mountbatten, and all those who mattered, were preparing their instruments for major surgery.

Before their decision impinged on our lives and everyone else's, we found a little freedom of our own, in an underground tunnel that we discovered below the third flat.

It was really part of an old, disused drainage system, and when Omar and I began exploring it, we had no idea just how far it extended. After crawling along on our bellies for some twenty feet, we found ourselves in complete darkness. Omar had brought along a small pencil torch, and with its help we continued writhing forward (moving backwards would have been quite impossible) until we saw a glimmer of light at the end of the tunnel. Dusty, musty, very scruffy, we emerged at last on to a grassy knoll, a little way outside the school boundary.

It's always a great thrill to escape beyond the boundaries that adults have devised. Here we were in unknown territory. To travel without passports—that would be the ultimate in freedom!

But more passports were on their way—and more boundaries.

Lord Mountbatten, viceroy and governor-general-to-be, came for our Founder's Day and gave away the prizes. I had won a prize for something or the other, and mounted the rostrum to receive my book from this towering, handsome man in his pinstripe suit. Bishop Cotton was then the premier school of India, often referred to as the 'Eton of the East'. Viceroys and governors had graced its functions. Many of its boys had gone on to eminence in the civil services and armed forces. There was one 'old boy' about whom they maintained a stolid silence—General Dyer, who had ordered the massacre at Amritsar and destroyed the trust that had been building up between Britain and India.

Now Mountbatten spoke of the momentous events that were happening all around us—the War had just come to an end, the United Nations held out the promise of a world living in peace and harmony, and India, an equal partner with Britain, would be among the great nations…

A few weeks later, Bengal and the Punjab provinces were bisected. Riots flared up across northern India, and there was a great exodus of people crossing the newly-drawn frontiers of Pakistan and India. Homes were destroyed, thousands lost their lives.

The common room radio and the occasional newspaper kept us abreast of events, but in our tunnel, Omar and I felt immune from all that was happening, worlds away from all the pillage, murder and revenge. And outside the tunnel, on the pine knoll below the school, there was fresh untrodden grass, sprinkled with clover and daisies; the only sounds we heard were the hammering of a woodpecker and the distant insistent call of the Himalayan Barbet. Who could touch us there?

'And when all the wars are done,' I said, 'a butterfly will still be beautiful.'

'Did you read that somewhere?'

'No, it just came into my head.'

'Already you're a writer.'

'No, I want to play hockey for India or football for Arsenal. Only winning teams!'

'You can't win forever. Better to be a writer.'

When the monsoon arrived, the tunnel was flooded, the drain choked with rubble. We were allowed out to the cinema to see Laurence Olivier's *Hamlet*, a film that did nothing to raise our spirits on a wet and gloomy afternoon; but it was our last picture that year, because communal riots suddenly broke out in Shimla's Lower Bazaar, an area that was still much as Kipling had described it—'a man who knows his way there can defy all the police of India's summer capital'—and we were confined to school indefinitely.

One morning after prayers in the chapel, the headmaster announced that the Muslim boys—those who had their homes in what was now Pakistan—would have to be evacuated, sent to their homes across the border with an armed convoy.

The tunnel no longer provided an escape for us. The bazaar was out of bounds. The flooded playing field was deserted. Omar and I sat on a damp wooden bench and talked about the future in vaguely hopeful terms, but we didn't solve any problems. Mountbatten and Nehru and Jinnah were doing all the solving.

It was soon time for Omar to leave—he left along with some fifty other boys from Lahore, Pindi and Peshawar. The rest of us—Hindus, Christians, Parsis—helped them load their luggage into the waiting trucks. A couple of boys broke down and wept. So did our departing school captain, a Pathan who had been known for his stoic and unemotional demeanour. Omar waved cheerfully to me and I waved back. We had vowed to meet again some day.

The convoy got through safely enough. There was only one casualty—the school cook, who had strayed into an off-limits area in the foothill town of Kalika and been set upon by a mob. He wasn't seen again.

Towards the end of the school year, just as we were all getting ready to leave for the school holidays, I received a letter from Omar. He told me something about his new school and how he missed my company and our games and our tunnel to freedom. I replied and gave him my home address, but I did not hear from him again.

Some seventeen or eighteen years later, I did get news of Omar, but in an entirely different context. India and Pakistan were at war, and in a bombing raid over Ambala, not far from Shimla, a Pakistani plane was shot down. Its crew died in the crash. One of them, I learnt later, was Omar.

Did he, I wonder, get a glimpse of the playing fields we knew so well as boys? Perhaps memories of his schooldays flooded back as he flew over the foothills. Perhaps he remembered the tunnel through which we were able to make our little escape to freedom.

But there are no tunnels in the sky.

The Last Tonga Ride

IT WAS a warm spring day in Dehradun, and the walls of the bungalow were aflame with flowering bougainvillea. The papayas were ripening. The scent of sweetpeas drifted across the garden. Grandmother sat in an easy chair in a shady corner of the veranda, her knitting needles clicking away, her head nodding now and then. She was knitting a pullover for my father. 'Delhi has cold winters,' she had said, and although the winter was still eight months away, she had set to work on getting our woollens ready.

In the Kathiawar states touched by the warm waters of the Arabian Sea, it had never been cold. But Dehra lies at the foot of the first range of the Himalayas.

Grandmother's hair was white and her eyes were not very strong, but her fingers moved quickly with the needles and the needles kept clicking all morning.

When Grandmother wasn't looking, I picked geranium leaves, crushed them between my fingers and pressed them to my nose.

I had been in Dehra with my grandmother for almost a month and I had not seen my father during this time. We had never before been separated for so long. He wrote to me every week, and sent me books and picture postcards, and I would walk to the end of the road to meet the postman as early as possible to see if there was any mail for us.

We heard the jingle of tonga bells at the gate and a familiar horse buggy came rattling up the drive.

'I'll see who's come,' I said, and ran down the veranda steps and across the garden.

It was Bansi Lal in his tonga. There were many tongas and tonga drivers in Dehra but Bansi was my favourite driver. He was young and handsome and he always wore a clean, white shirt and pyjamas. His pony, too, was bigger and faster than the other tonga ponies.

Bansi didn't have a passenger, so I asked him, 'What have you come for, Bansi?'

'Your grandmother sent for me, dost.' He did not call me 'Chota Sahib' or 'baba', but 'dost' and this made me feel much more important. Not every small boy could boast of a tonga driver for his friend!

'Where are you going, Granny?' I asked, after I had run back to the veranda.

'I'm going to the bank.'

'Can I come too?'

'Whatever for? What will you do in the bank?'

'Oh, I won't come inside, I'll sit in the tonga with Bansi.'

'Come along, then.'

We helped Grandmother into the back seat of the tonga, and then I joined Bansi in the driver's seat. He said something to his pony and the pony set off at a brisk trot, out of the gate and down the road.

'Now, not too fast, Bansi,' said grandmother, who didn't like anything that went too fast—tonga, motor car, train or bullock cart.

'Fast?' said Bansi. 'Have no fear, memsahib. This pony has never gone fast in its life. Even if a bomb went off behind us, we could go no faster. I have another pony which I use for racing when customers are in a hurry. This pony is reserved for you, memsahib.'

There was no other pony, but Grandmother did not know this, and was mollified by the assurance that she was riding in the slowest tonga in Dehra.

A ten-minute ride brought us to the bazaar. Grandmother's bank, the Allahabad Bank, stood near the clock tower. She was gone for about half an hour and during this period Bansi and I sauntered about in front of the shops. The pony had been left with some green stuff to munch.

'Do you have any money on you?' asked Bansi.

'Four annas,' I said.

'Just enough for two cups of tea,' said Bansi, putting his arm round my shoulders and guiding me towards a tea stall. The money passed from my palm to his.

'You can have tea, if you like,' I said. 'I'll have a lemonade.'

'So be it, friend. A tea and a lemonade, and be quick about it,' said Bansi to the boy in the tea shop and presently the drinks were set before us and Bansi was making a sound rather like his pony when it drank, while I burped my way through some green, gaseous stuff that tasted more like soap than lemonade.

When Grandmother came out of the bank, she looked pensive and did not talk much during the ride back to the house except to tell me to behave myself when I leant over to pat the pony on its rump. After paying off Bansi, she marched straight indoors.

'When will you come again?' I asked Bansi.

'When my services are required, dost. I have to make a living, you know. But I tell you what, since we are friends, the next time I am passing this way after leaving a fare, I will jingle my bells at the gate and if you are free and would like a ride—a fast ride!—you can join me. It won't cost you anything. Just bring some money for a cup of tea.'

'All right—since we are friends,' I said.

'Since we are friends.'

And touching the pony very lightly with the handle of his whip, he sent the tonga rattling up the drive and out of the gate. I could hear Bansi singing as the pony cantered down the road.

Ayah was waiting for me in the bedroom, her hands resting on her broad hips—sure sign of an approaching storm.

'So you went off to the bazaar without telling me,' she said. (It wasn't enough that I had Grandmother's permission!) 'And all this time I've been waiting to give you your bath.'

'It's too late now, isn't it?' I asked hopefully.

'No, it isn't. There's still an hour left for lunch. Off with your clothes!'

While I undressed, Ayah berated me for keeping the company of tonga drivers like Bansi. I think she was a little jealous.

'He is a rogue, that man. He drinks, gambles and smokes opium. He has TB and other terrible diseases. So don't you be too friendly with him, understand, baba?'

I nodded my head sagely but said nothing. I thought Ayah was exaggerating as she always did about people, and besides, I had no intention of giving up free tonga rides.

As my father had told me, Dehra was a good place for trees, and Grandmother's house was surrounded by several kinds—peepul, neem, mango, jackfruit, papaya and an ancient banyan tree. Some of the trees had been planted by my father and grandfather.

'How old is the jackfruit tree?' I asked Grandmother.

'Now let me see,' said Grandmother, looking very thoughtful. 'I should remember the jackfruit tree. Oh, yes, your grandfather put it down in 1927. It was during the rainy season. I remember because it was your father's birthday and we celebrated it by planting a tree—14 July 1927. Long before you were born!'

The banyan tree grew behind the house. Its spreading branches, which hung to the ground and took root again, formed a number of twisting passageways in which I liked to wander. The tree was older than the house, older than my grandparents, as old as Dehra. I could hide myself in its branches behind thick, green leaves and spy on the world below.

It was an enormous tree, about sixty feet high, and the first time I saw it I trembled with excitement because I had never seen such a marvellous tree before. I approached it slowly, even cautiously, as I wasn't sure the tree wanted my friendship. It looked as though it had many secrets. There were sounds and movements in the branches but I couldn't see who or what made the sounds.

The tree made the first move, the first overture of friendship. It allowed a leaf to fall.

The leaf brushed against my face as it floated down, but before it could reach the ground I caught and held it. I studied the leaf, running my fingers over its smooth, glossy texture. Then I put out my hand and touched the rough bark of the tree and this felt good to me. So I removed my shoes and socks as people do when they enter a holy place; and finding first a foothold and then a handhold on that broad trunk, I pulled myself up with the help of the tree's aerial roots.

As I climbed, it seemed as though someone was helping me. Invisible hands, the hands of the spirit in the tree, touched me and helped me climb.

But although the tree wanted me, there were others who were disturbed and alarmed by my arrival. A pair of parrots suddenly shot out of a hole in the trunk and with shrill cries, flew across the garden—flashes of green and red and gold. A squirrel looked out from behind a branch, saw me, and went scurrying away to inform his friends and relatives.

I climbed higher, looked up, and saw a red beak poised above my head. I shrank away, but the hornbill made no attempt to attack me. He was relaxing in his home, which was a great hole in the tree trunk. Only the bird's head and great beak were showing. He looked at me in rather a bored way, drowsily opening and shutting his eyes.

'So many creatures live here,' I said to myself. 'I hope none of them is dangerous!'

At that moment the hornbill lunged at a passing cricket. Bill and tree trunk met with a loud and resonant 'Tonk!'

I was so startled that I nearly fell out of the tree. But it was a difficult tree to fall out of! It was full of places where one could sit or even lie down. So I moved away from the hornbill, crawled along a branch which had sent out supports, and so moved quite a distance from the main body of the tree. I left its cold, dark depths for an area penetrated by shafts of sunlight.

No one could see me. I lay flat on the broad branch hidden by a screen of leaves. People passed by on the road below. A sahib in a sun helmet, his memsahib twirling a coloured silk sun umbrella. Obviously she did not want to get too brown and be mistaken for a country-born person. Behind them, a pram wheeled along by a nanny.

Then there were a number of Indians—some in white dhotis, some in western clothes, some in loincloths. Some with baskets on their heads. Others with coolies to carry their baskets for them.

A cloud of dust, the blare of a horn, and down the road, like an out-of-condition dragon, came the latest Morris touring car. Then cyclists. Then a man with a basket of papayas balanced on his head. Following him, a man with a performing monkey. This man rattled a little hand drum, and children followed man and monkey along the road. They stopped in the shade of a mango tree on the other side of the road. The little red monkey wore a frilled dress and a baby's bonnet. It danced for the children, while the man sang and played his drum.

The clip-clop of a tonga pony, and Bansi's tonga came rattling down the road. I called down to him and he reined in with a shout of surprise, and looked up into the branches of the banyan tree.

'What are you doing up there?' he cried.

'Hiding from Grandmother,' I said.

'And when are you coming for that ride?'

'On Tuesday afternoon,' I said.

'Why not today?'

'Ayah won't let me. But she has Tuesdays off.'

Bansi spat red paan juice across the road. 'Your ayah is jealous,' he said.

'I know,' I said. 'Women are always jealous, aren't they? I suppose it's because she doesn't have a tonga.'

'It's because she doesn't have a tonga driver,' said Bansi, grinning up at me. 'Never mind. I'll come on Tuesday—that's the day after tomorrow, isn't it?'

I nodded down to him, and then started backing along my branch, because I could hear Ayah calling in the distance. Bansi leant forward and smacked his pony across the rump, and the tonga shot forward.

'What were you doing up there?' asked Ayah a little later.

'I was watching a snake cross the road,' I said. I knew she couldn't resist talking about snakes. There weren't as many in Dehra as there had been in Kathiawar and she was thrilled that I had seen one.

'Was it moving towards you or away from you?' she asked.

'It was going away.'

Ayah's face clouded over. 'That means poverty for the beholder,' she said gloomily.

Later, while scrubbing me down in the bathroom, she began to air all her prejudices, which included drunkards ('they die quickly, anyway'), misers ('they get murdered sooner or later') and tonga drivers ('they have all the vices').

'You are a very lucky boy,' she said suddenly, peering closely at my tummy.

'Why?' I asked. 'You just said I would be poor because I saw a snake going the wrong way.'

'Well, you won't be poor for long. You have a mole on your tummy and that's very lucky. And there is one under your armpit, which means you will be famous. Do you have one on the neck? No, thank God! A mole on the neck is the sign of a murderer!'

'Do you have any moles?' I asked.

Ayah nodded seriously, and pulling her sleeve up to her shoulder, showed me a large mole high on her arm.

'What does that mean?' I asked.

'It means a life of great sadness,' said Ayah gloomily.

'Can I touch it?' I asked.

'Yes, touch it,' she said, and taking my hand, she placed it against the mole.

'It's a nice mole,' I said, wanting to make Ayah happy. 'Can I kiss it?'

'You can kiss it,' said Ayah.

I kissed her on the mole.

'That's nice,' she said.

Tuesday afternoon came at last, and as soon as Grandmother was asleep and Ayah had gone to the bazaar, I was at the gate, looking up and down the road for Bansi and his tonga. He was not long in coming. Before the tonga turned into the road,

I could hear his voice, singing to the accompaniment of the carriage bells.

He reached down, took my hand, and hoisted me on to the seat beside him. Then we went off down the road at a steady jogtrot. It was only when we reached the outskirts of the town that Bansi encouraged his pony to greater efforts. He rose in his seat, leaned forward and slapped the pony across the haunches. From a brisk trot we changed to a carefree canter. The tonga swayed from side to side. I clung to Bansi's free arm, while he grinned at me, his mouth red with paan juice.

'Where shall we go, dost?' he asked.

'Nowhere,' I said. 'Anywhere.'

'We'll go to the river,' said Bansi.

The 'river' was really a swift mountain stream that ran through the forests outside Dehra, joining the Ganga about fifteen miles away. It was almost dry during the winter and early summer; in flood during the monsoon.

The road out of Dehra was a gentle decline and soon we were rushing headlong through the tea gardens and eucalyptus forests, the pony's hoofs striking sparks off the metalled road, the carriage wheels groaning and creaking so loudly that I feared one of them would come off and that we would all be thrown into a ditch or into the small canal that ran beside the road. We swept through mango groves, through guava and litchi orchards, past broad-leaved sal and shisham trees. Once in the sal forest, Bansi turned the tonga on to a rough cart track, and we continued along it for about a furlong, until the road dipped down to the streambed.

'Let us go straight into the water,' said Bansi. 'You and I and the pony!' And he drove the tonga straight into the middle of the stream, where the water came up to the pony's knees.

'I am not a great one for baths,' said Bansi, 'but the pony

needs one, and why should a horse smell sweeter than its owner?' saying which, he flung off his clothes and jumped into the water.

'Better than bathing under a tap!' he cried, slapping himself on the chest and thighs. 'Come down, dost, and join me!'

After some hesitation I joined him, but had some difficulty in keeping on my feet in the fast current. I grabbed at the pony's tail and hung on to it, while Bansi began sloshing water over the patient animal's back.

After this, Bansi led both me and the pony out of the stream and together we gave the carriage a good washing down. I'd had a free ride and Bansi got the services of a free helper for the long overdue spring cleaning of his tonga. After we had finished the job, he presented me with a packet of aam papar—a sticky toffee made from mango pulp—and for some time I tore at it as a dog tears at a bit of old leather. Then I felt drowsy and lay down on the brown, sun-warmed grass. Crickets and grasshoppers were telephoning each other from tree and bush and a pair of blue jays rolled, dived, and swooped acrobatically overhead.

Bansi had no watch. He looked at the sun and said, 'It is past three. When will that ayah of yours be home? She is more frightening than your grandmother!'

'She comes at four.'

'Then we must hurry back. And don't tell her where we've been, or I'll never be able to come to your house again. Your grandmother's one of my best customers.'

'That means you'd be sorry if she died.'

'I would indeed, my friend.'

Bansi raced the tonga back to town. There was very little motor traffic in those days, and tongas and bullock carts were far more numerous than they are today.

We were back five minutes before Ayah returned. Before

Bansi left, he promised to take me for another ride the following week.

The house in Dehra had to be sold. My father had not left any money; he had never realized that his health would deteriorate so rapidly from the malarial fevers which had grown in frequency. He was still planning for the future when he died. Now that my father was gone, Grandmother saw no point in staying on in India; there was nothing left in the bank and she needed money for our passages to England, so the house had to go. Dr Ghose, who had a thriving medical practice in Dehra, made her a reasonable offer, which she accepted.

Then things happened very quickly. Grandmother sold most of our belongings, because as she said, we wouldn't be able to cope with a lot of luggage. The kabaris came in droves, buying up crockery, furniture, carpets and clocks at throwaway prices. Grandmother hated parting with some of her possessions such as the carved giltwood mirror, her walnut-wood armchair and her rosewood writing desk, but it was impossible to take them with us. They were carried away in a bullock cart.

Ayah was very unhappy at first but cheered up when Grandmother got her a job with a tea planter's family in Assam. It was arranged that she could stay with us until we left Dehra.

We went at the end of September, just as the monsoon clouds broke up, scattered, and were driven away by soft breezes from the Himalayas. There was no time to revisit the island where my father and I had planted our trees. And in the urgency and excitement of the preparations for our departure, I forgot to recover my small treasures from the hole in the banyan tree. It was only when we were in Bansi's tonga, on the way to the station, that I remembered my top, catapult and iron cross. Too late! To go back for them would mean missing the train.

'Hurry!' urged grandmother nervously. 'We mustn't be late for the train, Bansi.'

Bansi flicked the reins and shouted to his pony, and for once in her life Grandmother submitted to being carried along the road at a brisk trot.

'It's five to nine,' she said, 'and the train leaves at nine.'

'Do not worry, memsahib. I have been taking you to the station for fifteen years, and you have never missed a train!'

'No,' said Grandmother. 'And I don't suppose you'll ever take me to the station again, Bansi.'

'Times are changing, memsahib. Do you know that there is now a taxi—a motor car—competing with the tongas of Dehra? You are lucky to be leaving. If you stay, you will see me starve to death!'

'We will all starve to death if we don't catch that train,' said Grandmother.

'Do not worry about the train, it never leaves on time, and no one expects it to. If it left at nine o'clock, everyone would miss it.'

Bansi was right. We arrived at the station at five minutes past nine, and rushed on to the platform, only to find that the train had not yet arrived.

The platform was crowded with people waiting to catch the same train or to meet people arriving on it. Ayah was there already, standing guard over a pile of miscellaneous luggage. We sat down on our boxes and became part of the platform life at an Indian railway station.

Moving among piles of bedding and luggage were sweating, cursing coolies; vendors of magazines, sweetmeats, tea and betel-leaf preparations; also stray dogs, stray people and sometimes a stray stationmaster. The cries of the vendors mixed with the general clamour of the station and the shunting of a steam engine in the yards. 'Tea, hot tea!' Sweets, papads, hot stuff, cold drinks, toothpowder, pictures of film stars, bananas, balloons, wooden toys, clay images of the gods. The platform had become a bazaar.

Ayah was giving me all sorts of warnings.

'Remember, baba, don't lean out of the window when the train is moving. There was that American boy who lost his head last year! And don't eat rubbish at every station between here and Bombay. And see that no strangers enter the compartment. Mr Wilkins was murdered and robbed last year!'

The station bell clanged, and in the distance there appeared a big, puffing steam engine, painted green and gold and black. A stray dog with a lifetime's experience of trains, darted away across the railway lines. As the train came alongside the platform, doors opened, window shutters fell, faces appeared in the openings, and even before the train had come to a stop, people were trying to get in or out.

For a few moments there was chaos. The crowd surged backward and forward. No one could get out. No one could get in. A hundred people were leaving the train, two hundred were getting into it. No one wanted to give way.

The problem was solved by a man climbing out of a window. Others followed his example and the pressure at the doors eased and people started squeezing into their compartments.

Grandmother had taken the precaution of reserving berths in a first-class compartment, and assisted by Bansi and half-a-dozen coolies, we were soon inside with all our luggage. A whistle blasted and we were off! Bansi had to jump from the running train.

As the engine gathered speed, I ignored Ayah's advice and put my head out of the window to look back at the receding platform. Ayah and Bansi were standing on the platform waving to me, and I kept waving to them until the train rushed into the darkness and the bright lights of Dehra were swallowed up in the night. New lights, dim and flickering, came into existence as we passed small villages. The stars, too, were visible and I saw a shooting star streaking through the heavens.

I remembered something that Ayah had once told me, that stars are the spirits of good men, and I wondered if that shooting star was a sign from my father that he was aware of our departure and would be with us on our journey. And I remembered something else that Ayah had said—that if one wished on a shooting star, one's wish would be granted, provided, of course, that one thrust all five fingers into the mouth at the same time!

'What on earth are you doing?' asked Grandmother staring at me as I thrust my hand into my mouth.

'Making a wish,' I said.

'Oh,' said Grandmother.

She was preoccupied, and didn't ask me what I was wishing for; nor did I tell her.

*

The Night Train at Deoli

WHEN I was at college I used to spend my summer vacations in Dehra, at my grandmother's place. I would leave the plains early in May and return late in July. Deoli was a small station about thirty miles from Dehra. It marked the beginning of the heavy jungles of the Indian Terai.

The train would reach Deoli at about five in the morning when the station would be dimly lit with electric bulbs and oil lamps, and the jungle across the railway tracks would just be visible in the faint light of dawn. Deoli had only one platform, an office for the stationmaster and a waiting room. The platform boasted a tea stall, a fruit vendor and a few stray dogs; not much else because the train stopped there for only ten minutes before rushing on into the forests.

Why it stopped at Deoli, I don't know. Nothing ever happened there. Nobody got off the train and nobody got on. There were never any coolies on the platform. But the train would halt there a full ten minutes and then a bell would sound, the guard would blow his whistle, and presently Deoli would be left behind and forgotten.

I used to wonder what happened in Deoli behind the station walls. I always felt sorry for that lonely little platform and for the place that nobody wanted to visit. I decided that one day I would get off the train at Deoli and spend the day there just to please the town.

I was eighteen, visiting my grandmother, and the night train stopped at Deoli. A girl came down the platform selling baskets.

It was a cold morning and the girl had a shawl thrown across her shoulders. Her feet were bare and her clothes were old but she was a young girl, walking gracefully and with dignity.

When she came to my window, she stopped. She saw that I was looking at her intently, but at first she pretended not to notice. She had pale skin, set off by shiny black hair and dark, troubled eyes. And then those eyes, searching and eloquent, met mine.

She stood by my window for some time and neither of us said anything. But when she moved on, I found myself leaving my seat and going to the carriage door. I stood waiting on the platform looking the other way. I walked across to the tea stall. A kettle was boiling over on a small fire, but the owner of the stall was busy serving tea somewhere on the train. The girl followed me behind the stall.

'Do you want to buy a basket?' she asked. 'They are very strong, made of the finest cane...'

'No,' I said, 'I don't want a basket.'

We stood looking at each other for what seemed a very long time, and she said, 'Are you sure you don't want a basket?'

'All right, give me one,' I said, and took the one on top and gave her a rupee, hardly daring to touch her fingers.

As she was about to speak, the guard blew his whistle. She said something, but it was lost in the clanging of the bell and the hissing of the engine. I had to run back to my compartment. The carriage shuddered and jolted forward.

I watched her as the platform slipped away. She was alone on the platform and she did not move, but she was looking at me and smiling. I watched her until the signal box came in the way and then the jungle hid the station. But I could still see her standing there alone...

I stayed awake for the rest of the journey. I could not rid my mind of the picture of the girl's face and her dark, smouldering eyes.

But when I reached Dehra the incident became blurred and distant, for there were other things to occupy my mind. It was only when I was making the return journey, two months later, that I remembered the girl.

I was looking out for her as the train drew into the station, and I felt an unexpected thrill when I saw her walking up the platform. I sprang off the footboard and waved to her.

When she saw me, she smiled. She was pleased that I remembered her. I was pleased that she remembered me. We were both pleased and it was almost like a meeting of old friends.

She did not go down the length of the train selling baskets but came straight to the tea stall. Her dark eyes were suddenly filled with light. We said nothing for some time but we couldn't have been more eloquent.

I felt the impulse to put her on the train there and then, and take her away with me. I could not bear the thought of having to watch her recede into the distance of Deoli station. I took the baskets from her hand and put them down on the ground. She put out her hand for one of them, but I caught her hand and held it.

'I have to go to Delhi,' I said.

She nodded. 'I do not have to go anywhere.'

The guard blew his whistle for the train to leave, and how I hated the guard for doing that.

'I will come again,' I said. 'Will you be here?'

She nodded again and, as she nodded, the bell clanged and the train slid forward. I had to wrench my hand away from the girl and run for the moving train.

This time I did not forget her. She was with me for the

remainder of the journey and for long after. All that year she was a bright, living thing. And when the college term finished, I packed in haste and left for Dehra earlier than usual. My grandmother would be pleased at my eagerness to see her.

I was nervous and anxious as the train drew into Deoli, because I was wondering what I should say to the girl and what I should do. I was determined that I wouldn't stand helplessly before her, hardly able to speak or do anything about my feelings.

The train came to Deoli, and I looked up and down the platform but I could not see the girl anywhere.

I opened the door and stepped off the footboard. I was deeply disappointed and overcome by a sense of foreboding. I felt I had to do something and so I ran up to the stationmaster and said, 'Do you know the girl who used to sell baskets here?'

'No, I don't,' said the stationmaster. 'And you'd better get on the train if you don't want to be left behind.'

But I paced up and down the platform and stared over the railings at the station yard. All I saw was a mango tree and a dusty road leading into the jungle. Where did the road go? The train was moving out of the station and I had to run up the platform and jump for the door of my compartment. Then, as the train gathered speed and rushed through the forests, I sat brooding in front of the window.

What could I do about finding a girl I had seen only twice, who had hardly spoken to me, and about whom I knew nothing—absolutely nothing—but for whom I felt a tenderness and responsibility that I had never felt before?

My grandmother was not pleased with my visit after all, because I didn't stay at her place more than a couple of weeks. I felt restless and ill at ease. So I took the train back to the plains, meaning to ask further questions of the stationmaster at Deoli.

But at Deoli there was a new stationmaster. The previous man had been transferred to another post within the past week. The new man didn't know anything about the girl who sold baskets. I found the owner of the tea stall, a small, shrivelled-up man, wearing greasy clothes, and asked him if he knew anything about the girl with the baskets.

'Yes, there was such a girl here. I remember quite well,' he said. 'But she has stopped coming now.'

'Why?' I asked. 'What happened to her?' 'How should I know?' said the man. 'She was nothing to me.' And once again I had to run for the train. As Deoli platform receded, I decided that one day I would have to break journey there, spend a day in the town, make inquiries, and find the girl who had stolen my heart with nothing but a look from her dark, impatient eyes.

With this thought I consoled myself throughout my last term in college. I went to Dehra again in the summer and when, in the early hours of the morning, the night train drew into Deoli station, I looked up and down the platform for signs of the girl, knowing I wouldn't find her but hoping just the same.

Somehow, I couldn't bring myself to break journey at Deoli and spend a day there. (If it was all fiction or a film, I reflected, I would have got down and cleaned up the mystery and reached a suitable ending to the whole thing.) I think I was afraid to do this. I was afraid of discovering what really happened to the girl. Perhaps she was no longer in Deoli, perhaps she was married, perhaps she had fallen ill...

In the last few years I have passed through Deoli many times, and I always look out of the carriage window half expecting to see the same unchanged face smiling up at me. I wonder what happens in Deoli, behind the station walls. But I will never break my journey there. It may spoil my game. I prefer to keep hoping and dreaming and looking out of the window up and down that lonely platform, waiting for the girl with the baskets.

I never break my journey at Deoli but I pass through as often as I can.

ƒ

The Coral Tree

THE NIGHT had been hot, the rain frequent, and I had been sleeping on the verandah instead of in the house. I was in my twenties, had begun to earn a living and felt I had certain responsibilities.

In a short time, a tonga would take me to the railway station, and from there a train would take me to Bombay, and then a ship would take me to England. There would be work, interviews, a job, a different kind of life, so many things that this small bungalow of my grandfather would be remembered fitfully, in rare moments of reflection.

When I awoke on the veranda, I saw a grey morning, smelt the rain on the red earth and remembered that I had to go away. A girl was standing on the veranda porch, looking at me very seriously. When I saw her, I sat up in bed with a start.

She was a small dark girl, her eyes big and black, her pigtails tied up in a bright red ribbon, and she was fresh and clean like the rain and the red earth.

She stood looking at me and was very serious.

'Hullo,' I said, smiling and trying to put her at ease. But the girl was business-like and acknowledged my greeting with a brief nod.

'Can I do anything for you?' I asked, stretching my limbs. 'Do you stay nearby?'

With great assurance she said, 'Yes, but I can stay on my own.'

'You're like me,' I said, and for a while, forgot about being an old man of twenty. 'I like to be on my own but I'm going away today.'

'Oh,' she said, a little breathlessly.

'Would you care to go to England?'

'I want to go everywhere,' she said. 'To America and Africa and Japan and Honolulu.'

'Maybe you will,' I said. 'I'm going everywhere, and no one can stop me... But what is it you want, what did you come for?'

'I want some flowers but I can't reach them.' She waved her hand towards the garden, 'That tree, see?'

The coral tree stood in front of the house surrounded by pools of water and broken, fallen blossoms. The branches of the tree were thick with scarlet, pea-shaped flowers.

'All right, just let me get ready.'

The tree was easy to climb and I made myself comfortable on one of the lower branches, smiling down at the serious upturned face of the girl.

'I'll throw them down to you,' I said.

I bent a branch but the wood was young and green and I had to twist it several times before it snapped.

'I'm not sure I ought to do this,' I said as I dropped the flowering branch to the girl.

'Don't worry,' she said.

I felt a sudden nostalgic longing for childhood and an urge to remain behind in my grandfather's house with its tangled memories and ghosts of yesteryear. But I was the only one left and what could I do except climb tamarind and jackfruit trees?

'Have you many friends?' I asked.

'Oh yes.'

'And who is the best?'

'The cook. He lets me stay in the kitchen which is more

interesting than the house. And I like to watch him cooking. And he gives me things to eat and tells me stories...'

'And who is your second best friend?'

She inclined her head to one side and thought very hard. 'I'll make you second best,' she said.

I sprinkled coral blossoms on her head. 'That's very kind of you. I'm happy to be second best.'

A tonga bell sounded at the gate and I looked out from the tree and said, 'It's come for me. I have to go now.'

I climbed down.

'Will you help me with my suitcases?' I asked, as we walked together towards the veranda. 'There's no one here to help me. I am the last to go. Not because I want to go but because I have to.'

I sat down on the cot and packed a few last things in my suitcase. All the doors of the house were locked. On my way to the station, I would leave the keys with the caretaker. I had already given instructions to the agent to try and sell the house. There was nothing more to be done. We walked in silence to the waiting tonga, thinking and wondering about each other. The girl stood at the side of the path, on the damp earth, looking at me.

'Thank you,' I said, 'I hope I shall see you again.'

'I'll see you in London,' she said. 'Or America or Japan, I want to go everywhere.'

'I'm sure you will,' I said. 'And perhaps I'll come back and we'll meet again in this garden. That would be nice, wouldn't it?'

She nodded and smiled. We knew it was an important moment. The tonga driver spoke to his pony and the carriage set off down the gravel path, rattling a little. The girl and I waved to each other. In the girl's hand was a sprig of coral blossom. As she waved, the blossoms fell apart and danced lightly in the breeze.

'Goodbye!' I called.

'Goodbye!' called the girl.

The ribbon had come loose from her pigtail and lay on the ground with the coral blossoms.

And she was fresh and clean like the rain and the red earth.

ƒ

Love and Cricket

IT WAS a quiet day in New Delhi. Everyone was indoors, watching an India-Pakistan cricket match on TV. Even the hotel seemed understaffed. I'd given up on cricket years ago, after a long and uninteresting career as twelfth man for the Chutmalpur Club team. Carrying out the drinks or fielding in the hot sun on behalf of others had finally soured my attitude towards the game. Now my greatest pleasure was sitting in a shady spot, sipping a cool drink brought to me by an agile young waiter, who would no doubt have preferred to be out on a cricket field.

It was an elderly waiter who brought me the nimbu-pani. The younger ones were probably crowded around a TV set in the kitchen. I relaxed in the easy chair of the hotel's garden restaurant, here I was an occasional customer. Sweet-peas filled the air with their heady perfume. Snapdragons snapped in the mid-March sunshine. A carpet of soft pink phlox was soothing to the eyes. New Delhi in the spring is kind to flower gardens.

I had the place to myself. I felt at peace with the world. The garden was quiet and restful—until two noisy children, a boy who must have been about twelve, and a girl a little younger, came charging out of the shadows, kicking a rubber ball around. Having played football myself once, I looked at their game with amused tolerance; that is, until the boy, bending it like Beckham, sent the ball crashing on to my table, upsetting my nimbu-pani.

The elderly waiter came running to my rescue. The children

fled concealing themselves behind some potted palms. Their mother appeared on the steps, threatening them with dire consequences. She walked over to me, apologizing. 'I'm so sorry. They are very naughty.' 'That's all right,' I said, 'just high spirits. And it seems to be the season for ball games.'

The sun was in my eyes and I couldn't see her very well. She was about forty, on the plump side, dark and quite attractive. 'It's perfectly all right,' I said again, as the waiter brought me another nimbu-pani.

She just stood there, staring at me 'Weren't you—aren't you—Rusty?'

I looked at her more closely then. It was a long time since anyone had called me Rusty. I stood up so that the sun wouldn't be in my eyes. There was something about *her* eyes, soft and gentle, and her hair, still lustrous, and her lips of course, that reminded me of—

'Sushila?' I said hesitantly. Could it really be her—grown chubby and middle-aged and maternal? Sushila, my lost love of twenty plus years ago...

'Yes, I am Sushila. And you are Rusty. A little older now.

'And grown quite rusty over the years.' I took her hand and asked her to join me. 'And call the children over.' But the children had made themselves scarce.

'They must have gone to play video games.' She sat down without any hesitation. 'It will be nice to talk to you. It's so boring staying in these big hotels.'

I called the waiter over and she ordered an orange drink. I raised my glass and looked at her through the translucent liquid. She had worn well with the years—much better than I had! Although youth had flown, vestiges of youthfulness remained in her dimpled smile, full lips and lively glance. Her once slim hand was now a chubby hand; but all the same, it would be nice to touch it, and I did so, allowing my fingers to rest lightly against her palm. She drew her hand away, but not too quickly.

'So, now you're a mother of two,' I remarked, by way of making conversation.

'Three,' she said. 'My eldest boy is at boarding. He's fifteen. You never married?'

'Not after you turned me down.'

'I did not turn you down. It was my parents' wish.'

'I know. It wasn't your fault—and it wasn't theirs. I had no money, and no prospects. It wouldn't have been fair to you. And I would have had to give up my writing and take some miserable job.'

'Would you have done that for me?'

'Of course, I loved you.'

'But now you are successful. Had you married me, you would not be so well-known.'

'Who knows? I might have done better. Your husband must be very successful to be staying here.'

'Ah, but he's in business. In Bombay, a stockbroker. I know nothing about it. I'm just a housewife.'

'Well, three children must keep you pretty busy.'

We were silent for some time. Traffic hummed along nearby Janpath, but it was quiet in the garden. You could even hear the cooing of doves from the verandah roof. A hoopoe hopped across the grass, looking for insects.

Twenty years ago we had held hands and walked barefoot across the grass on the little hillock overlooking the stream that tumbled down to Mossy Falls. I still have photographs taken that day. Her cousin had gone paddling downstream, looking for coloured pebbles, and I had taken advantage of his absence by kissing her, first on the cheeks, and then, quite suddenly, on the lips.

Now she seemed to be recalling the same incident because she said, 'You were very romantic, Rusty.'

'I'm still romantic. But the modern world has no time for romance. It's all done on computers now. Make love by e-mail. It's much safer.'

'And you preferred the moonlight.'

'Ah, those full moon nights, do you remember them? The moon coming up over the top of Landour, and then pouring through the windows of Maplewood... And you put your head against my shoulder and I held you there until a cloud came across the moon. And then you let me kiss you everywhere.'

'I don't remember that.'

'Of course you do.'

'What happened to your bicycle? The one you used to sing about.'

'The bicycle went the way of all machines. There were others. But the song still lingers on. My grandfather used to sing it to my grandmother, before they were married. There it is—.' And I sang it again, softly, with the old waiter listening intently in the background:

> *Daisy, Daisy, give me your answer, do!*
> *I'm half crazy all for the love of you!*
> *It won't be a stylish marriage,*
> *As I can't afford a carriage,*
> *But you'll look sweet upon the seat*
> *Of a bicycle built for two.*

Sushila laughed and clapped her hands. The waiter smiled and nodded his approval.

'And your grandparents—were they happy with a bicycle?'

'Very happy. That's all they had for years. But I see you have a new BMW. Very nice.'

The children were waving to her from a parked car. 'We have to go shopping,' she said. 'But not until the match is over.'

'Well, it's only lunch time. The game will finish at five.'

Something buzzed in her handbag, and she opened it and took out a mobile. Yes, my dear old Sushila, simple sweetheart of my youth, was now equipped with the latest technology. She listened carefully to what someone was saying, then switched off with a look of resignation.

'No shopping?' I asked.

'No shopping. He bet on Tendulkar making a duck.'

'And what did he score?'

'A hundred. My husband lost a lakh. It's nothing. Would you like to have lunch with us? It's so boring here.'

'No,' I said. 'I have to go.'

'Back to your lonely cottage, in the hills?'

'Yes, eventually. I come here sometimes, when I'm in Delhi. I like the flower garden. But I'm staying with friends.' As I got up to go, she gave me her hand.

'Will you come again?'

'I can't say. But it was great meeting you, Sushila. You look lovelier than ever. Even when you're bored.'

I gave the waiter a generous tip, and he followed me out to the parking lot and very respectfully dusted off the seat of my bicycle. I wobbled down the road to Janpath, humming the tune of that well-remembered song.

✶

The Night the Roof Blew off

WE ARE used to sudden storms up here on the first range of the Himalayas. The old building in which we live has, for more than a hundred years, received the full force of the wind as it sweeps across the hills from the east.

We'd lived in the building for more than ten years without a disaster. It had even taken the shock of a severe earthquake. As my granddaughter Dolly said, 'It's difficult to tell the new cracks from the old!'

It's a two-storey building, and I live on the upper floor with my family: my three grandchildren and their parents. The roof is made of corrugated tin sheets, the ceiling of wooden boards. That's the traditional Mussoorie roof.

Looking back at the experience, it was the sort of thing that should have happened in a James Thurber story, like the dam that burst or the ghost who got in. But I wasn't thinking of Thurber at the time, although a few of his books were among the many I was trying to save from the icy rain pouring into my bedroom.

Our roof had held fast in many a storm, but the wind that night was really fierce. It came rushing at us with a high-pitched, eerie wail. The old roof groaned and protested. It took a battering for several hours while the rain lashed against the windows and the lights kept coming and going.

There was no question of sleeping, but we remained in bed for warmth and comfort. The fire had long since gone out as the chimney had collapsed, bringing down a shower of sooty rainwater.

After about four hours of buffeting, the roof could take it no longer. My bedroom faces east, so my portion of the roof was the first to go.

The wind got under it and kept pushing until, with a ripping, groaning sound, the metal sheets shifted and slid off the rafters, some of them dropping with claps like thunder on to the road below.

So that's it, I thought. Nothing worse can happen. As long as the ceiling stays on, I'm not getting out of bed. We'll collect our roof in the morning.

Icy water splashing down on my face made me change my mind in a hurry. Leaping from the bed, I found that much of the ceiling had gone, too. Water was pouring on my open typewriter as well as on the bedside radio and bed cover.

Picking up my precious typewriter (my companion for forty years), I stumbled into the front sitting room (and library), only to find a similar situation there. Water was pouring through the slats of the wooden ceiling, raining down on the open bookshelves.

By now I had been joined by the children, who had come to my rescue. Their section of the roof hadn't gone as yet. Their parents were struggling to close a window against the driving rain.

'Save the books!' shouted Dolly, the youngest, and that became our rallying cry for the next hour or two.

Dolly and her brother Mukesh picked up armfuls of books and carried them into their room. But the floor was awash, so the books had to be piled on their beds. Dolly was helping me gather some of my papers when a large field rat jumped on to the desk in front of her. Dolly squealed and ran for the door.

'It's all right,' said Mukesh, whose love of animals extends even to field rats. 'It's only sheltering from the storm.'

Big brother Rakesh whistled for our dog, Tony, but Tony wasn't interested in rats just then. He had taken shelter in the kitchen, the only dry spot in the house.

Two rooms were now practically roofless, and we could see the sky lit up by flashes of lightning.

There were fireworks indoors, too, as water spluttered and crackled along a damaged wire. Then the lights went out altogether.

Rakesh, at his best in an emergency, had already lit two kerosene lamps. And by their light we continued to transfer books, papers, and clothes to the children's room.

We noticed that the water on the floor was beginning to subside a little.

'Where is it going?' asked Dolly.

'Through the floor,' said Mukesh. 'Down to the flat below!'

Cries of concern from our downstairs neighbours told us that they were having their share of the flood.

Our feet were freezing because there hadn't been time to put on proper footwear. And besides, shoes and slippers were awash by now. All chairs and tables were piled high with books. I hadn't realized the extent of my library until that night!

The available beds were pushed into the driest corner of the children's room, and there, huddled in blankets and quilts, we spent the remaining hours of the night while the storm continued.

Towards morning the wind fell, and it began to snow. Through the door to the sitting room I could see snowflakes drifting through the gaps in the ceiling, settling on picture frames. Ordinary things like a glue bottle and a small clock took on a certain beauty when covered with soft snow.

Most of us dozed off.

When dawn came, we found the windowpanes encrusted

with snow and icicles. The rising sun struck through the gaps in the ceiling and turned everything golden. Snow crystals glistened on the empty bookshelves. But the books had been saved.

Rakesh went out to find a carpenter and tinsmith, while the rest of us started putting things in the sun to dry. By evening, we'd put much of the roof back on.

It's a much-improved roof now, and we look forward to the next storm with confidence!

The Photograph

I WAS ten years old. My grandmother sat on the string bed under the mango tree. It was late summer and there were sunflowers in the garden and a warm wind in the trees. My grandmother was knitting a woollen scarf for the winter months. She was very old, dressed in a plain white sari. Her eyes were not very strong now but her fingers moved quickly with the needles and the needles kept clicking all afternoon. Grandmother had white hair but there were very few wrinkles on her skin.

I had come home after playing cricket on the maidan. I had taken my meal and now I was rummaging through a box of old books and family heirlooms that had just that day been brought out of the attic by my mother. Nothing in the box interested me very much except for a book with colourful pictures of birds and butterflies. I was going through the book, looking at the pictures, when I found a small photograph between the pages. It was a faded picture, a little yellow and foggy. It was the picture of a girl standing against a wall and behind the wall there was nothing but sky. But from the other side a pair of hands reached up, as though someone was going to climb the wall. There were flowers growing near the girl but I couldn't tell what they were. There was a creeper too but it was just a creeper.

I ran out into the garden. 'Granny!' I shouted. 'Look at this picture! I found it in the box of old things. Whose picture is it?'

I jumped on the bed beside my grandmother and she

walloped me on the bottom and said, 'Now I've lost count of my stitches and the next time you do that I'll make you finish the scarf yourself.'

Granny was always threatening to teach me how to knit which I thought was a disgraceful thing for a boy to do. It was a good deterrent for keeping me out of mischief. Once I had torn the drawing-room curtains and Granny had put a needle and thread in my hand and made me stitch the curtain together, even though I made long, two-inch stitches, which had to be taken out by my mother and done again.

She took the photograph from my hand and we both stared at it for quite a long time. The girl had long, loose hair and she wore a long dress that nearly covered her ankles, and sleeves that reached her wrists, and there were a lot of bangles on her hands. But despite all this drapery, the girl appeared to be full of freedom and movement. She stood with her legs apart and her hands on her hips and had a wide, almost devilish smile on her face.

'Whose picture is it?' I asked.

'A little girl's, of course,' said Grandmother. 'Can't you tell?'

'Yes, but did you know the girl?'

'Yes, I knew her,' said Granny, 'but she was a very wicked girl and I shouldn't tell you about her. But I'll tell you about the photograph. It was taken in your grandfather's house about sixty years ago. And that's the garden wall and over the wall there was a road going to town.'

'Whose hands are they,' I asked, 'coming up from the other side?'

Grandmother squinted and looked closely at the picture, and shook her head. 'It's the first time I've noticed,' she said. 'They must have been the sweeper boy's. Or maybe they were your grandfather's.'

'They don't look like Grandfather's hands,' I said. 'His hands are all bony.'

'Yes, but this was sixty years ago.'

'Didn't he climb up the wall after the photo?'

'No, nobody climbed up. At least, I don't remember.'

'And you remember well, Granny.'

'Yes, I remember... I remember what is not in the photograph. It was a spring day and there was a cool breeze blowing, nothing like this. Those flowers at the girl's feet, they were marigolds, and the bougainvillea creeper, it was a mass of purple. You cannot see these colours in the photo and even if you could, as nowadays, you wouldn't be able to smell the flowers or feel the breeze.'

'And what about the girl?' I said. 'Tell me about the girl.'

'Well, she was a wicked girl,' said Granny. 'You don't know the trouble they had getting her into those fine clothes she's wearing.'

'I think they are terrible clothes,' I said.

'So did she. Most of the time, she hardly wore a thing. She used to go swimming in a muddy pool with a lot of ruffianly boys, and ride on the backs of buffaloes. No boy ever teased her, though, because she could kick and scratch and pull his hair out!'

'She looks like it too,' I said. 'You can tell by the way she's smiling. At any moment something's going to happen.'

'Something did happen,' said Granny. 'Her mother wouldn't let her take off the clothes afterwards, so she went swimming in them and lay for half an hour in the mud.'

I laughed heartily and Grandmother laughed too.

'Who was the girl?' I said. 'You must tell me who she was.'

'No, that wouldn't do,' said Grandmother, but I pretended I didn't know. I knew, because Grandmother still smiled in the same way, even though she didn't have as many teeth.

'Come on, Granny,' I said, 'tell me, tell me.'

But Grandmother shook her head and carried on with the knitting. And I held the photograph in my hand looking from it to my Grandmother and back again, trying to find points in common between the old lady and the little pigtailed girl. A lemon-coloured butterfly settled on the end of grandmother's knitting needle and stayed there while the needles clicked away. I made a grab at the butterfly and it flew off in a dipping flight and settled on a sunflower.

'I wonder whose hands they were,' whispered Grandmother to herself, with her head bowed, and her needles clicking away in the soft, warm silence of that summer afternoon.

The Tunnel

It was almost noon, and the jungle was very still, very silent. Heat waves shimmered along the railway embankment where it cut a path through the tall evergreen trees. The railway lines were two straight black serpents disappearing into the tunnel in the hillside.

Suraj stood near the cutting, waiting for the midday train. It wasn't a station, and he wasn't catching a train. He was waiting so that he could watch the steam engine come roaring out of the tunnel.

He had cycled out of Dehra and taken the jungle path until he had come to a small village. He had left the cycle there, and walked over a low scrub-covered hill and down to the tunnel exit.

Now he looked up. He had heard, in the distance, the shrill whistle of the engine. He couldn't see anything, because the train was approaching from the other side of the hill; but presently a sound like distant thunder issued from the tunnel, and he knew the train was coming through.

A second or two later, the steam engine shot out of the tunnel, snorting and puffing like some green, black and gold dragon, some beautiful monster out of Suraj's dreams. Showering sparks left and right, it roared a challenge to the jungle.

Instinctively, Suraj stepped back a few paces. Waves of hot steam struck him in the face. Even the trees seemed to flinch from the noise and heat. And then the train had gone, leaving only a plume of smoke to drift lazily over the tall shisham trees.

The jungle was still again. No one moved.

Suraj turned from his contemplation of the drifting smoke and began walking along the embankment towards the tunnel.

The tunnel grew darker as he walked further into it. When he had gone about twenty yards, it became pitch dark. Suraj had to turn and look back at the opening to reassure himself that there was still daylight outside. Ahead of him, the tunnel's other opening was just a small round circle of light.

The tunnel was still full of smoke from the train, but it would be several hours before another train came through. Till then, the cutting belonged to the jungle again.

Suraj didn't stop, because there was nothing to do in the tunnel and nothing to see. He had simply wanted to walk through, so that he would know what the inside of a tunnel was really like. The walls were damp and sticky. A bat flew past. A lizard scuttled between the lines.

Coming straight from the darkness into the light, Suraj was dazzled by the sudden glare and put a hand up to shade his eyes. He looked up at the tree-covered hillside and thought he saw something moving between the trees.

It was just a flash of orange and gold, and a long swishing tail. It was there between the trees for a second or two, and then it was gone.

About fifteen metres from the entrance to the tunnel stood the watchman's hut. Marigolds grew in front of the hut, and at the back there was a small vegetable patch. It was the watchman's duty to inspect the tunnel and keep it clear of obstacles. Every day, before the train came through, he would walk the length of the tunnel. If all was well, he would return to his hut and take a nap. If something was wrong, he would walk back up the line and wave a red flag and the engine driver would slow down. At night, the watchman lit an oil lamp and made a similar inspection of the tunnel. Of course, he would not stop the train if there was a porcupine on the line. But if there was any danger to the train, he'd go back up the line and wave his lamp to the approaching engine. If all was well, he'd hang his lamp at the door of his hut and go to sleep.

He was just settling down on his cot for an afternoon nap when he saw the boy emerge from the tunnel. He waited until Suraj was only a metre or so away and then said: 'Welcome, welcome. I don't often have visitors. Sit down for a while, and tell me why you were inspecting my tunnel.'

'Is it your tunnel?' asked Suraj.

'It is,' said the watchman. 'It is truly my tunnel, since no one else will have anything to do with it. I have only lent it to the Government.'

Suraj sat down on the edge of the cot.

'I wanted to see the train come through,' he said. 'And then, when it had gone, I thought I'd walk through the tunnel.'

'And what did you find in it?'

'Nothing. It was very dark. But when I came out, I thought I saw an animal—up on the hill—but I'm not sure, it moved off very quickly.'

'It was a leopard you saw,' said the watchman. 'My leopard.'

'Do you own a leopard too?'

'I do.'

'And do you lend it to the Government?'

'I do not.'

'Is it dangerous?'

'No, it's a leopard that minds its own business. It comes to this range for a few days every month.'

'Have you been here a long time?' asked Suraj.

'Many years. My name is Sunder Singh.'

'My name's Suraj.'

'There is one train during the day. And there is one train during the night. Have you seen the night mail come through the tunnel?'

'No. At what time does it come?'

'About nine o'clock, if it isn't late. You could come and sit here with me, if you like. And after it has gone, instead of going to sleep I will take you home.'

'I'll ask my parents,' said Suraj. 'Will it be safe?'

'Of course. It is safer in the jungle than in the town. Nothing happens to me out here. But last month, when I went into town, I was almost run over by a bus.'

Sunder Singh yawned and stretched himself out on the cot. 'And now I am going to take a nap, my friend. It is too hot to be up and about in the afternoon.'

'Everyone goes to sleep in the afternoon,' complained Suraj. 'My father lies down as soon as he's had his lunch.'

'Well, the animals also rest in the heat of the day. It is only the tribe of boys who cannot, or will not, rest.'

Sunder Singh placed a large banana leaf over his face to keep away the flies, and was soon snoring gently. Suraj stood up, looking up and down the railway tracks. Then he began walking back to the village.

The following evening, towards dusk, as the flying foxes swooped silently out of the trees, Suraj made his way to the watchman's hut.

It had been a long hot day, but now the earth was cooling, and a light breeze was moving through the trees. It carried with it the scent of mango blossoms, the promise of rain.

Sunder Singh was waiting for Suraj. He had watered his small garden, and the flowers looked cool and fresh. A kettle was boiling on a small oil stove.

'I am making tea,' he said. 'There is nothing like a glass of hot tea while waiting for a train.'

They drank their tea, listening to the sharp notes of the tailorbird and the noisy chatter of the seven sisters.

As the brief twilight faded, most of the birds fell silent. Sunder Singh lit his oil lamp and said it was time for him to inspect the tunnel. He moved off towards the tunnel, while Suraj sat on the cot, sipping his tea. In the dark, the trees seemed to move closer to him. And the nightlife of the forest was conveyed on the breeze—the sharp call of a barking deer, the cry of a fox, the quaint tonk-tonk of a nightjar. There were some sounds that Suraj didn't recognize—sounds that came from the trees, creakings and whisperings, as though the trees were coming to life, stretching their limbs in the dark, shifting a little, flexing their fingers.

Sunder Singh stood inside the tunnel, trimming his lamp. The night sounds were familiar to him and he did not give them much thought; but something else—a padded footfall, a rustle of dry leaves—made him stand still for a few seconds, peering into the darkness. Then, humming softly to himself, he returned to where Suraj was waiting. Ten minutes remained for the night mail to arrive.

As Sunder Singh sat down on the cot beside Suraj, a new sound reached both of them quite distinctly—a rhythmic sawing sound, as of someone cutting through the branch of a tree.

'What's that?' whispered Suraj.

'It's the leopard,' said Sunder Singh. 'I think it's in the tunnel.'

'The train will soon be here,' said Suraj.

'Yes, my friend. And if we don't drive the leopard out of the tunnel, it will be run over and killed. I can't let that happen.'

'But won't it attack us if we try to drive it out?' asked Suraj, beginning to share the watchman's concern.

'Not this leopard. It knows me well. We have seen each other many times. It has a weakness for goats and stray dogs, but it will not harm us. Even so, I'll take my axe with me. You stay here, Suraj.'

'No, I'm coming with you. It will be better than sitting here alone in the dark!'

'All right, but stay close behind me. And remember, there is nothing to fear.'

Raising his lamp, Sunder Singh advanced into the tunnel, shouting at the top of his voice to try and scare away the animal. Suraj followed close behind; but he found he was unable to do any shouting. His throat was quite dry.

They had gone about twenty paces into the tunnel when the light from the lamp fell upon the leopard. It was crouching between the tracks, only five metres away from them. It was not a very big leopard, but it looked lithe and sinewy. Baring its teeth and snarling, it went down on its belly, tail twitching.

Suraj and Sunder Singh both shouted together. Their voices rang through the tunnel. And the leopard, uncertain as to how many terrifying humans were there in the tunnel with him, turned swiftly and disappeared into the darkness.

To make sure that it had gone, Sunder Singh and Suraj walked the length of the tunnel. When they returned to the entrance, the rails were beginning to hum. They knew the train was coming.

Suraj put his hand to one of the rails and felt its tremor. He heard the distant rumble of the train. And then the engine came round the bend, hissing at them, scattering sparks into the darkness, defying the jungle as it roared through the steep sides of the cutting. It charged straight at the tunnel, and into it, thundering past Suraj like the beautiful dragon of his dreams.

And when it had gone, the silence returned and the forest seemed to breathe, to live again. Only the rails still trembled with the passing of the train.

They trembled again to the passing of the same train, almost a week later, when Suraj and his father were both travelling in it.

Suraj's father was scribbling in a notebook, doing his accounts. Suraj sat at an open window staring out at the darkness. His father was going to Delhi on a business trip and had decided to take the boy along. ('I don't know where he gets to, most of the time,' he'd complained. 'I think it's time he learnt something about my business.')

The night mail rushed through the forest with its hundreds of passengers. The carriage wheels beat out a steady rhythm on the rails. Tiny flickering lights came and went, as they passed small villages on the fringe of the jungle.

Suraj heard the rumble as the train passed over a small bridge. It was too dark to see the hut near the cutting, but he knew they must be approaching the tunnel. He strained his eyes looking out into the night; and then, just as the engine let out a shrill whistle, Suraj saw the lamp.

He couldn't see Sunder Singh, but he saw the lamp, and he knew that his friend was out there.

The train went into the tunnel and out again; it left the jungle behind and thundered across the endless plains.

Suraj stared out at the darkness, thinking of the lonely cutting in the forest and the watchman with the lamp who would always remain a firefly for those travelling thousands as he lit up the darkness for steam engines and leopards.

✦

The Overcoat

Iᴛ ᴡᴀs clear frosty weather, and as the moon came up over the Himalayan peaks, I could see that patches of snow still lay on the roads of the hill-station. I would have been quite happy in bed, with a book and a hot-water bottle at my side, but I'd promised the Kapadias that I'd go to their party, and I felt it would be churlish of me to stay away. I put on two sweaters, an old football scarf and an overcoat, and set off down the moonlit road.

It was a walk of just over a mile to the Kapadias' house, and I had covered about half the distance when I saw a girl standing in the middle of the road.

She must have been sixteen or seventeen. She looked rather old-fashioned—long hair, hanging to her waist, and a flummoxy sequined dress, pink and lavender, that reminded me of the photos in my grandmother's family album. When I went closer, I noticed that she had lovely eyes and a winning smile.

'Good evening,' I said. 'It's a cold night to be out.' 'Are you going to the party?' she asked.

'That's right. And I can see from your lovely dress that you're going, too. Come along, we're nearly there.'

She fell into step beside me and we soon saw lights from the Kapadias' house shining brightly through the deodars. The girl told me her name was Julie. I hadn't seen her before but, then, I'd only been in the hill-station a few months.

There was quite a crowd at the party, and no one seemed to know Julie. Everyone thought she was a friend of mine. I did not deny it. Obviously she was someone who was feeling lonely and wanted to be friendly with people. And she was certainly enjoying herself. I did not see her do much eating or drinking but she flitted about from one group to another, talking, listening, laughing; and when the music began, she was dancing almost continuously, alone or with partners, it didn't matter which, she was completely wrapped up in the music.

It was almost midnight when I got up to go. I had drunk a fair amount of punch, and I was ready for bed. As I was saying goodnight to my hosts and wishing everyone a Merry Christmas, Julie slipped her arm into mine and said she'd be going home, too. When we were outside I said, 'Where do you live, Julie?' 'At Wolfsburn,' she said. 'At the top of the hill.' 'There's a cold wind,' I said. And although your dress is beautiful, it doesn't look very warm. Here, you'd better wear my overcoat. I've plenty of protection.'

She did not protest, and allowed me to slip my overcoat over her shoulders. Then we started out on the walk home. But I did not have to escort her all the way. At about the spot where we had met, she said, 'There's a short cut from here. I'll just scramble up the hillside.'

'Do you know it well?' I asked. 'It's a very narrow path.'

'Oh, I know every stone on the path. I use it all the time. And besides, it's a really bright night.'

'Well, keep the coat on,' I said. 'I can collect it tomorrow.'

She hesitated for a moment, then smiled and nodded to me. She then disappeared up the hill, and I went home alone.

The next day I walked up to Wolfsburn. I crossed a little brook, from which the house had probably got its name, and entered an open iron gate. But of the house itself little remained. Just a roofless ruin, a pile of stones, a shattered chimney, a few Doric pillars where a verandah had once stood.

Had Julie played a joke on me? Or had I found the wrong house?

I walked around the hill to the mission house where the Taylors lived, and asked old Mrs Taylor if she knew a girl called Julie.

'No, I don't think so,' she said. 'Where does she live?' 'At Wolfsburn, I was told. But the house is just a ruin.'

'Nobody has lived at Wolfsburn for over forty years. The Mackinnons lived there. One of the old families who settled here. But when their girl died...' She stopped and gave me a queer look. 'I think her name was Julie... Anyway, when she died, they sold the house and went away. No one ever lived in it again, and it fell into decay. But it couldn't be the same Julie you're looking for. She died of consumption—there wasn't much you could do about it in those days. Her grave is in the cemetery, just down the road.'

I thanked Mrs Taylor and walked slowly down the road to the cemetery: not really wanting to know any more, but propelled forward almost against my will.

It was a small cemetery under the deodars. You could see the eternal snows of the Himalayas standing out against the pristine blue of the sky. Here lay the bones of forgotten Empire-builders—soldiers, merchants, adventurers, their wives and children. It did not take me long to find Julie's grave. It had a simple headstone with her name clearly outlined on it:

Julie Mackinnon
1923–39
With us one moment,
Taken the next.
Gone to her Maker,
Gone to her rest.

Although many monsoons had swept across the cemetery wearing down the stones, they had not touched this little tombstone.

I was turning to leave when I caught a glimpse of something familiar behind the headstone. I walked round to where it lay.

Neatly folded on the grass was my overcoat.

✗

The Girl on the Train

I HAD the train compartment to myself up to Rohana, then a girl got in. The couple who saw her off were probably her parents; they seemed very anxious about her comfort, and the woman gave the girl detailed instructions as to where to keep her things, when not to lean out of windows, and how to avoid speaking to strangers.

They called their goodbyes and the train pulled out of the station. As I was going blind at the time, my eyes sensitive only to light and darkness, I was unable to tell what the girl looked like; but I knew she wore slippers from the way they slapped against her heels.

It would take me some time to discover something about her looks, and perhaps I never would. But I liked the sound of her voice, and even the sound of her slippers.

'Are you going all the way to Dehra?' I asked.

I must have been sitting in a dark corner, because my voice startled her. She gave a little exclamation and said, 'I didn't know anyone else was here.'

Well, it often happens that people with good eyesight fail to see what is right in front of them. They have too much to take in, I suppose. Whereas people who cannot see (or see very little) have to take in only the essentials, whatever registers most tellingly on their remaining senses.

'I didn't see you either,' I said. 'But I heard you come in.'

I wondered if I would be able to prevent her from discovering that I was blind. Provided I keep to my seat, I thought, it shouldn't be too difficult.

The girl said, 'I'm getting off at Saharanpur. My aunt is meeting me there.'

'Then I had better not get too familiar,' I replied. 'Aunts are usually formidable creatures.'

'Where are you going?' she asked.

'To Dehra, and then to Mussoorie.'

'Oh, how lucky you are. I wish I were going to Mussoorie. I love the hills. Especially in October.'

'Yes, this is the best time,' I said, calling on my memories. 'The hills are covered with wild dahlias, the sun is delicious, and at night you can sit in front of a logfire and drink a little brandy. Most of the tourists have gone, and the roads are quiet and almost deserted. Yes, October is the best time.'

She was silent. I wondered if my words had touched her, or whether she thought me a romantic fool. Then I made a mistake.

'What is it like outside?' I asked.

She seemed to find nothing strange in the question. Had she noticed already that I could not see? But her next question removed my doubts.

'Why don't you look out of the window?' she asked.

I moved easily along the berth and felt for the window ledge. The window was open, and I faced it, making a pretence of studying the landscape. I heard the panting of the engine, the rumble of the wheels, and, in my mind's eye, I could see telegraph posts flashing by.

'Have you noticed,' I ventured, 'that the trees seem to be moving while we seem to be standing still?'

'That always happens,' she said. 'Do you see any animals?'

'No,' I answered quite confidently. I knew that there were hardly any animals left in the forests near Dehra.

I turned from the window and faced the girl, and for a while we sat in silence.

'You have an interesting face,' I remarked. I was becoming quite daring, but it was a safe remark. Few girls can resist flattery. She laughed pleasantly—a clear ringing laugh.

'It's nice to be told I have an interesting face. I'm tired of people telling me I have a pretty face.'

Oh, so you do have a pretty face, thought I; and aloud I said, 'Well, an interesting face can also be pretty.'

'You are a very gallant young man,' she said 'but why are you so serious?'

I thought, then, I would try to laugh for her, but the thought of laughter only made me feel troubled and lonely.

'We'll soon be at your station,' I said.

'Thank goodness it's a short journey. I can't bear to sit in a train for more than two or three hours.'

Yet I was prepared to sit there for almost any length of time, just to listen to her talking. Her voice had the sparkle of a mountain stream. As soon as she left the train, she would forget our brief encounter; but it would stay with me for the rest or the journey, and for some time after.

The engine's whistle shrieked, the carriage wheels changed their sound and rhythm, the girl got up and began to collect her things. I wondered if she wore her hair in a bun, or if it was plaited; perhaps it was hanging loose over her shoulders, or was it cut very short?

The train drew slowly into the station. Outside, there was the shouting of porters and vendors and a high-pitched female voice near the carriage door; that voice must have belonged to the girl's aunt.

'Goodbye,' the girl said.

She was standing very close to me, so close that the perfume from her hair was tantalizing. I wanted to raise my hand and touch her hair, but she moved away. Only the scent of perfume still lingered where she had stood.

There was some confusion in the doorway. A man, getting into the compartment, stammered an apology. Then the door banged, and the world was shut out again. I returned to my berth. The guard blew his whistle and we moved off. Once again, I had a game to play and a new fellow-traveller.

The train gathered speed, the wheels took up their song, the carriage groaned and shook. I found the window and sat in front of it, staring into the daylight that was darkness for me.

So many things were happening outside the window: it could be a fascinating game, guessing what went on out there.

The man who had entered the compartment broke into my reverie.

'You must be disappointed,' he said. 'I'm not nearly as attractive a travelling companion as the one who just left.'

'She was an interesting girl,' I said. 'Can you tell me—did she keep her hair long or short?'

'I don't remember,' he said, sounding puzzled. 'It was her eyes I noticed, not her hair. She had beautiful eyes—but they were of no use to her. She was completely blind. Didn't you notice?'

*

The Woman on Platform No. 8

IT WAS my second year at boarding school, and I was sitting on platform no. 8 at Ambala station, waiting for the northern bound train. I think I was about twelve at the time. My parents considered me old enough to travel alone, and I had arrived by bus at Ambala early in the evening; now there was a wait till midnight before my train arrived. Most of the time I had been pacing up and down the platform, browsing through the bookstall, or feeding broken biscuits to stray dogs; trains came and went, the platform would be quiet for a while and then, when a train arrived, it would be an inferno of heaving, shouting, agitated human bodies. As the carriage doors opened, a tide of people would sweep down upon the nervous little ticket collector at the gate; and every time this happened I would be caught in the rush and swept outside the station. Now tired of this game and of ambling about the platform, I sat down on my suitcase and gazed dismally across the railway tracks.

Trolleys rolled past me, and I was conscious of the cries of the various vendors—the men who sold curds and lemon, the sweetmeat seller, the newspaper boy—but I had lost interest in all that was going on along the busy platform, and continued to stare across the railway tracks, feeling bored and a little lonely.

'Are you all alone, my son?' asked a soft voice close behind me.

I looked up and saw a woman standing near me. She was leaning over, and I saw a pale face and dark kind eyes. She wore no jewels, and was dressed very simply in a white sari.

'Yes, I am going to school,' I said, and stood up respectfully. She seemed poor, but there was a dignity about her that commanded respect.

'I have been watching you for some time,' she said. 'Didn't your parents come to see you off?'

'I don't live here,' I said. 'I had to change trains. Anyway, I can travel alone.'

'I am sure you can,' she said, and I liked her for saying that, and I also liked her for the simplicity of her dress, and for her deep, soft voice and the serenity of her face. 'Tell me, what is your name?' she asked. 'Arun,' I said.

'And how long do you have to wait for your train?' 'About an hour, I think. It comes at twelve o'clock.' 'Then come with me and have something to eat.' I was going to refuse, out of shyness and suspicion, but she took me by the hand, and then I felt it would be silly to pull my hand away. She told a coolie to look after my suitcase, and then she led me away down the platform. Her hand was gentle, and she held mine neither too firmly nor too lightly. I looked up at her again. She was not young. And she was not old. She must have been over thirty, but had she been fifty, I think she would have looked much the same.

She took me into the station dining room, ordered tea and samosas and jalebis, and at once I began to thaw and take a new interest in this kind woman. The strange encounter had little effect on my appetite. I was a hungry school boy, and I ate as much as I could in as polite a manner as possible. She took obvious pleasure in watching me eat, and I think it was the food that strengthened the bond between us and cemented our friendship, for under the influence of the tea and sweets I began to talk quite freely, and told her about my school, my friends, my likes and dislikes. She questioned me quietly from time to time, but preferred listening; she drew me out very well, and I had soon forgotten that we were strangers. But she did not ask me about my family or where I lived, and I did not ask her where she lived. I accepted her for what she had been to me—a quiet, kind and gentle woman who gave sweets to a lonely boy on a railway platform...

After about half an hour we left the dining room and began walking back along the platform. An engine was shunting up and down beside platform no. 8, and as it approached, a boy leapt off the platform and ran across the rails, taking a short cut to the next platform. He was at a safe distance from the engine, but as he leapt across the rails, the woman clutched my arm. Her fingers dug into my flesh, and I winced with pain. I caught her fingers and looked up at her, and I saw a spasm of pain and fear and sadness pass across her face. She watched the boy as he climbed the platform, and it was not until he had disappeared in the crowd that she relaxed her hold on my arm. She smiled at me reassuringly and took my hand again, but her fingers trembled against mine.

'He was all right,' I said, feeling that it was she who needed reassurance.

She smiled gratefully at me and pressed my hand. We walked together in silence until we reached the place where I had left my suitcase. One of my schoolfellows, Satish, a boy of about my age, had turned up with his mother.

'Hello, Arun!' he called. 'The train's coming in late, as usual. Did you know we have a new headmaster this year?'

We shook hands, and then he turned to his mother and said: 'This is Arun, Mother. He is one of my friends, and the best bowler in the class.'

'I am glad to know that,' said his mother, a large imposing

woman who wore spectacles. She looked at the woman who held my hand and said: 'And I suppose you're Arun's mother?'

I opened my mouth to make some explanation, but before I could say anything the woman replied: 'Yes, I am Arun's mother.'

I was unable to speak a word. I looked quickly up at the woman, but she did not appear to be at all embarrassed, and was smiling at Satish's mother.

Satish's mother said: 'It's such a nuisance having to wait for the train right in the middle of the night. But one can't let the child wait here alone. Anything can happen to a boy at a big station like this—there are so many suspicious characters hanging about. These days one has to be very careful of strangers.'

'Arun can travel alone though,' said the woman beside me, and somehow I felt grateful to her for saying that. I had already forgiven her for lying; and besides, I had taken an instinctive dislike to Satish's mother.

'Well, be very careful, Arun,' said Satish's mother looking sternly at me through her spectacles. 'Be very careful when your mother is not with you. And never talk to strangers!'

I looked from Satish's mother to the woman who had given me tea and sweets, and back at Satish's mother.

'I like strangers,' I said.

Satish's mother definitely staggered a little, as obviously she was not used to being contradicted by small boys. 'There you are, you see! If you don't watch over them all the time, they'll walk straight into trouble. Always listen to what your mother tells you,' she said, wagging a fat little finger at me. 'And never, never talk to strangers.'

I glared resentfully at her, and moved closer to the woman who had befriended me. Satish was standing behind his mother, grinning at me, and delighting in my clash with his mother. Apparently he was on my side.

The station bell clanged, and the people who had till now been squatting resignedly on the platform began bustling about.

'Here it comes,' shouted Satish, as the engine whistle shrieked and the front lights played over the rails.

The train moved slowly into the station, the engine hissing and sending out waves of steam. As it came to a stop, Satish jumped on the footboard of a lighted compartment and shouted, 'Come on, Arun, this one's empty!' and I picked up my suitcase and made a dash for the open door.

We placed ourselves at the open windows, and the two women stood outside on the platform, talking up to us. Satish's mother did most of the talking.

'Now don't jump on and off moving trains, as you did just now,' she said. 'And don't stick your heads out of the windows, and don't eat any rubbish on the way.' She allowed me to share the benefit of her advice, as she probably didn't think my 'mother' a very capable person. She handed Satish a bag of fruit, a cricket bat and a big box of chocolates, and told him to share the food with me. Then she stood back from the window to watch how my 'mother' behaved.

I was smarting under the patronizing tone of Satish's mother, who obviously thought mine a very poor family; and I did not intend giving the other woman away. I let her take my hand in hers, but I could think of nothing to say. I was conscious of Satish's mother staring at us with hard, beady eyes, and I found myself hating her with a firm, unreasoning hate. The guard walked up the platform, blowing his whistle for the train to leave. I looked straight into the eyes of the woman who held my hand, and she smiled in a gentle, understanding way. I leaned out of the window then, and put my lips to her cheek and kissed her.

The carriage jolted forward, and she drew her hand away.

'Goodbye, Mother!' said Satish, as the train began to move slowly out of the station. Satish and his mother waved to each other.

'Goodbye,' I said to the other woman, 'goodbye—Mother…' I didn't wave or shout, but sat still in front of the window, gazing at the woman on the platform. Satish's mother was talking to her, but she didn't appear to be listening; she was looking at me, as the train took me away. She stood there on the busy platform, a pale sweet woman in white, and I watched her until she was lost in the milling crowd.

The Fight

Ranji had been less than a month in Rajpur when he discovered the pool in the forest. It was the height of summer, and his school had not yet opened, and, having as yet made no friends in this semi-hill station, he wandered about a good deal by himself into the hills and forests that stretched away interminably on all sides of the town. It was hot, very hot, at that time of year, and Ranji walked about in his vest and shorts, his brown feet white with the chalky dust that flew up from the ground. The earth was parched, the grass brown, the trees listless, hardly stirring, waiting for a cool wind or a refreshing shower of rain.

It was on such a day—a hot, tired day—that Ranji found the pool in the forest. The water had a gentle translucency, and you could see the smooth round pebbles at the bottom of the pool. A small stream emerged from a cluster of rocks to feed the pool. During the monsoon, this stream would be a gushing torrent, cascading down from the hills, but during the summer it was barely a trickle. The rocks, however, held the water in the pool, and it did not dry up like the pools in the plains.

When Ranji saw the pool, he did not hesitate to get into it. He had often gone swimming, alone or with friends, when he had lived with his parents in a thirsty town in the middle of the Rajputana desert. There, he had known only sticky, muddy pools, where buffaloes wallowed and women washed clothes. He had never seen a pool like this—so clean and cold and inviting. He threw off all his clothes, as he had done when he went swimming in the plains, and leapt into the water. His limbs were supple, free of any fat, and his dark body glistened in patches of sunlit water.

The next day he came again to quench his body in the cool waters of the forest pool. He was there for almost an hour, sliding in and out of the limpid green water, or lying stretched out on the smooth yellow rocks in the shade of broad-leaved sal trees. It was while he lay thus, naked on a rock, that he noticed another boy standing a little distance away, staring at him in a rather hostile manner. The other boy was a little older than Ranji, taller, thickset, with a broad nose and thick, red lips. He had only just noticed Ranji, and he stood at the edge of the pool, wearing a pair of bathing shorts, waiting for Ranji to explain himself.

When Ranji did not say anything, the other called out, 'What are you doing here, Mister?'

Ranji, who was prepared to be friendly, was taken aback at the hostility of the other's tone.

'I am swimming,' he replied. 'Why don't you join me?'

'I always swim alone,' said the other. 'This is my pool, I did not invite you here. And why are you not wearing any clothes?'

'It is not your business if I do not wear clothes. I have nothing to be ashamed of.'

'You skinny fellow, put on your clothes.'

'Fat fool, take yours off.'

This was too much for the stranger to tolerate. He strode up to Ranji, who still sat on the rock and, planting his broad feet firmly on the sand, said (as though this would settle the matter once and for all), 'Don't you know I am a Punjabi? I do not take replies from villagers like you!'

'So you like to fight with villagers?' said Ranji. 'Well, I am not a villager. I am a Rajput!'

'I am a Punjabi!'

'I am a Rajput!'

They had reached an impasse. One had said he was a Punjabi, the other had proclaimed himself a Rajput. There was little else that could be said.

'You understand that I am a Punjabi?' said the stranger, feeling that perhaps this information had not penetrated Ranji's head.

'I have heard you say it three times,' replied Ranji.

'Then why are you not running away?'

'I am waiting for *you* to run away!'

'I will have to beat you,' said the stranger, assuming a violent attitude, showing Ranji the palm of his hand.

'I am waiting to see you do it,' said Ranji.

'You will see me do it,' said the other boy.

Ranji waited. The other boy made a strange, hissing sound. They stared each other in the eye for almost a minute. Then the Punjabi boy slapped Ranji across the face with all the force he could muster. Ranji staggered, feeling quite dizzy. There were thick red finger marks on his cheek.

'There you are!' exclaimed his assailant. 'Will you be off now?'

For answer, Ranji swung his arm up and pushed a hard, bony fist into the other's face.

And then they were at each other's throats, swaying on the rock, tumbling on to the sand, rolling over and over, their legs and arms locked in a desperate, violent struggle. Gasping and cursing, clawing and slapping, they rolled right into the shallows of the pool.

Even in the water the fight continued as, spluttering and covered with mud, they groped for each other's head and throat. But after five minutes of frenzied, unscientific struggle, neither boy had emerged victorious. Their bodies heaving with exhaustion, they stood back from each other, making tremendous efforts to speak.

'Now—now do you realize—I am a Punjabi?' gasped the stranger.

'Do you know I am a Rajput?' said Ranji with difficulty.

They gave a moment's consideration to each other's answers, and in that moment of silence there was only their heavy breathing and the rapid beating of their hearts.

'Then you will not leave the pool?' said the Punjabi boy.

'I will not leave it,' said Ranji.

'Then we shall have to continue the fight,' said the other.

'All right,' said Ranji.

But neither boy moved, neither took the initiative.

The Punjabi boy had an inspiration.

'We will continue the fight tomorrow,' he said. 'If you dare to come here again tomorrow, we will continue this fight, and I will not show you mercy as I have done today.'

'I will come tomorrow,' said Ranji. 'I will be ready for you.'

They turned from each other then and, going to their respective rocks, put on their clothes, and left the forest by different routes.

When Ranji got home, he found it difficult to explain the cuts and bruises that showed on his face, legs and arms. It was difficult to conceal the fact that he had been in an unusually violent fight, and his mother insisted on his staying at home for the rest of the day. That evening, though, he slipped out of the house and went to the bazaar, where he found comfort and solace in a bottle of vividly coloured lemonade and a banana leaf full of hot, sweet jalebis. He had just finished the lemonade when he saw his adversary coming down the road. His first impulse was to turn away and look elsewhere, his second to throw the lemonade bottle at his enemy. But he did neither of these things. Instead, he stood his ground and scowled at his passing adversary. And the Punjabi boy said nothing either, but scowled back with equal ferocity.

The next day was as hot as the previous one. Ranji felt weak and lazy and not at all eager for a fight. His body was stiff and sore after the previous day's encounter. But he could not refuse the challenge. Not to turn up at the pool would be an acknowledgement of defeat. From the way he felt just then, he knew he would be beaten in another fight. But he could not acquiesce in his own defeat. He must defy his enemy to the last, or outwit him, for only then could he gain his respect. If he surrendered now, he would be beaten for all time; but to fight and be beaten today left him free to fight and be beaten again. As long as he fought, he had a right to the pool in the forest.

He was half hoping that the Punjabi boy would have forgotten the challenge, but these hopes were dashed when he saw his opponent sitting, stripped to the waist, on a rock on the other side of the pool. The Punjabi boy was rubbing oil on his body, massaging it into his broad thighs. He saw Ranji beneath the sal trees, and called a challenge across the waters of the pool.

'Come over on this side and fight!' he shouted.

But Ranji was not going to submit to any conditions laid down by his opponent.

'Come *this* side and fight!' he shouted back with equal vigour.

'Swim across and fight me here!' called the other. 'Or perhaps you cannot swim the length of this pool?'

But Ranji could have swum the length of the pool a dozen times without tiring, and here he would show the Punjabi boy his superiority. So, slipping out of his vest and shorts, he dived straight into the water, cutting through it like a knife, and surfaced with hardly a splash. The Punjabi boy's mouth hung open in amazement.

'You can dive!' he exclaimed.

'It is easy,' said Ranji, treading water, waiting for a further challenge. 'Can't you dive?'

'No,' said the other. 'I jump straight in. But if you will tell me how, I will make a dive.'

'It is easy,' said Ranji. 'Stand on the rock, stretch your arms out and allow your head to displace your feet.'

The Punjabi boy stood up, stiff and straight, stretched out his arms, and threw himself into the water. He landed flat on his belly, with a crash that sent the birds screaming out of the trees.

Ranji dissolved into laughter.

'Are you trying to empty the pool?' he asked, as the Punjabi boy came to the surface, spouting water like a small whale.

'Wasn't it good?' asked the boy, evidently proud of his feat.

'Not very good,' said Ranji. 'You should have more practice. See, I will do it again.'

And pulling himself up on a rock, he executed another perfect dive. The other boy waited for him to come up, but, swimming under water, Ranji circled him and came upon him from behind.

'How did you do that?' asked the astonished youth.

'Can't you swim under water?' asked Ranji.

'No, but I will try it.'

The Punjabi boy made a tremendous effort to plunge to the bottom of the pool and indeed he thought he had gone right down, though his bottom, like a duck's, remained above the surface.

Ranji, however, did not discourage him.

'It was not bad,' he said. 'But you need a lot of practice.'

'Will you teach me?' asked his enemy.

'If you like, I will teach you.'

'You must teach me. If you do not teach me, I will beat

you. Will you come here every day and teach me?'

'If you like,' said Ranji. They had pulled themselves out of the water, and were sitting side by side on a smooth grey rock.

'My name is Suraj,' said the Punjabi boy. 'What is yours?'

'It is Ranji.'

'I am strong, am I not?' asked Suraj, bending his arm so that a ball of muscle stood up stretching the white of his flesh.

'You are strong,' said Ranji. 'You are a real pehelwan.'

'One day I will be the world's champion wrestler,' said Suraj, slapping his thighs, which shook with the impact of his hand. He looked critically at Ranji's hard, thin body. 'You are quite strong yourself,' he conceded. 'But you are too bony. I know, you people do not eat enough. You must come and have your food with me. I drink one seer of milk every day. We have got our own cow! Be my friend, and I will make you a pehelwan like me! I know—if you teach me to dive and swim under water, I will make you a pehelwan! That is fair, isn't it?'

'That is fair!' said Ranji, though he doubted if he was getting the better of the exchange.

Suraj put his arm around the younger boy and said, 'We are friends now, yes?'

They looked at each other with honest, unflinching eyes, and in that moment love and understanding were born.

'We are friends,' said Ranji.

The birds had settled again in their branches, and the pool was quiet and limpid in the shade of the sal trees.

'It is our pool,' said Suraj. 'Nobody else can come here without our permission. Who would dare?'

'Who would dare?' said Ranji, smiling with the knowledge that he had won the day.

✦

A Long Walk for Bina

1

A LEOPARD, lithe and sinewy, drank at the mountain stream, and then lay down on the grass to bask in the late February sunshine. Its tail twitched occasionally and the animal appeared to be sleeping. At the sound of distant voices it raised its head to listen, then stood up and leapt lightly over the boulders in the stream, disappearing among the trees on the opposite bank.

A minute or two later, three children came walking down the forest path. They were a girl and two boys, and they were singing in their local dialect an old song they had learnt from their grandparents.

Five more miles to go!
We climb through rain and snow.
A river to cross...
A mountain to pass...
Now we've four more miles to go!

Their school satchels looked new, their clothes had been washed and pressed. Their loud and cheerful singing startled a Spotted Forktail. The bird left its favourite rock in the stream and flew down the dark ravine.

'Well, we have only three more miles to go,' said the bigger boy, Prakash, who had been this way hundreds of times. 'But first we have to cross the stream.'

He was a sturdy twelve-year-old with eyes like black currants and a mop of bushy hair that refused to settle down on his head. The girl and her small brother were taking this path for the first time.

'I'm feeling tired, Bina,' said the little boy.

Bina smiled at him, and Prakash said, 'Don't worry, Sonu, you'll get used to the walk. There's plenty of time.' He glanced at the old watch he'd been given by his grandfather. It needed constant winding. 'We can rest here for five or six minutes.'

They sat down on a smooth boulder and watched the clear water of the shallow stream tumbling downhill. Bina examined the old watch on Prakash's wrist. The glass was badly scratched and she could barely make out the figure on the dial. 'Are you sure it still gives the right time?' she asked.

'Well, it loses five minutes every day, so I put it ten minutes forward at night. That means by morning it's quite accurate! Even our teacher, Mr Mani, asks me for the time. If he doesn't ask, I tell him! The clock in our classroom keeps stopping.'

They removed their shoes and let the cold mountain water run over their feet. Bina was the same age as Prakash. She had pink cheeks, soft brown eyes, and hair that was just beginning to lose its natural curls. Hers was a gentle face, but a determined little chin showed that she could be a strong person. Sonu, her younger brother, was ten. He was a thin boy who had been sickly as a child but was now beginning to fill out. Although he did not look very athletic, he could run like the wind.

■

Bina had been going to school in her own village of Koli, on the other side of the mountain. But it had been a Primary School, finishing at Class 5. Now, in order to study in the Class 6, she would have to walk several miles every day to Nauti, where there was a High School going up to Class 8. It had been decided that Sonu would also shift to the new school, to give Bina company. Prakash, their neighbour in Koli, was already a pupil at the Nauti school. His mischievous nature, which sometimes got him into trouble, had resulted in his having to repeat a year.

But this didn't seem to bother him. 'What's the hurry?' he had told his indignant parents. 'You're not sending me to a foreign land when I finish school. And our cows aren't running away, are they?'

'You would prefer to look after the cows, wouldn't you?' asked Bina, as they got up to continue their walk.

'Oh, school's all right. Wait till you see old Mr Mani. He always gets our names mixed up, as well as the subjects he's supposed to be teaching. At our last lesson, instead of maths, he gave us a geography lesson!'

'More fun than maths,' said Bina.

'Yes, but there's a new teacher this year. She's very young they say, just out of college. I wonder what she'll be like.'

Bina walked faster and Sonu had some trouble keeping up with them. She was excited about the new school and the prospect of different surroundings. She had seldom been outside her own village, with its small school and single ration shop. The day's routine never varied—helping her mother in the fields or with household tasks like fetching water from the spring or cutting grass and fodder for the cattle. Her father, who was a soldier, was away for nine months in the year and Sonu was still too small for the heavier tasks.

As they neared Nauti village, they were joined by other children coming from different directions. Even where there were no major roads, the mountains were full of little lanes and shortcuts. Like a game of snakes and ladders, these narrow paths zigzagged around the hills and villages, cutting through fields and crossing narrow ravines until they came together to form a fairly busy road along which mules, cattle and goats joined the throng.

Nauti was a fairly large village, and from here a broader but dustier road started for Tehri. There was a small bus, several trucks and (for part of the way) a road roller. The road hadn't been completed because the heavy diesel roller couldn't take the steep climb to Nauti. It stood on the roadside halfway up the road from Tehri.

Prakash knew almost everyone in the area, and exchanged greetings and gossip with other children as well as with muleteers, bus drivers, milkmen and labourers working on the road. He loved telling everyone the time, even if they weren't interested.

'It's nine o'clock,' he would announce, glancing at his wrist. 'Isn't your bus leaving today?'

'Off with you!' the bus driver would respond, 'I'll leave when I'm ready.'

As the children approached Nauti, the small flat school buildings came into view on the outskirts of the village, fringed by a line of long-leaved pines. A small crowd had assembled on the one playing field. Something unusual seemed to have happened. Prakash ran forward to see what it was all about. Bina and Sonu stood aside, waiting in a patch of sunlight near the boundary wall.

Prakash soon came running back to them. He was bubbling over with excitement.

'It's Mr Mani!' he gasped. 'He's disappeared! People are saying a leopard must have carried him off!'

2

Mr Mani wasn't really old. He was about fifty-five and was expected to retire soon. But for the children, most adults over forty seemed ancient! And Mr Mani had always been a bit absent-minded, even as a young man.

He had gone out for his early morning walk, saying he'd be back by eight o'clock, in time to have his breakfast and be ready for class. He wasn't married, but his sister and her husband stayed with him. When it was past nine o'clock his sister presumed he'd stopped at a neighbour's house for breakfast (he loved tucking into other people's breakfast) and that he had gone on to school from there. But when the school bell rang at ten o'clock, and everyone but Mr Mani was present, questions were asked and guesses were made.

No one had seen him return from his walk and enquiries made in the village showed that he had not stopped at anyone's house. For Mr Mani to disappear was puzzling; for him to disappear without his breakfast was extraordinary.

Then a milkman returning from the next village said he had seen a leopard sitting on a rock on the outskirts of the pine forest. There had been talk of a cattle-killer in the valley, of leopards and other animals being displaced by the constructions of a dam. But as yet no one had heard of a leopard attacking a man. Could Mr Mani have been its first victim? Someone found a strip of red cloth entangled in a blackberry bush and went running through the village showing it to everyone. Mr Mani had been known to wear red pyjamas. Surely he had been seized and eaten! But where were his remains? And why had he been in his pyjamas?

Meanwhile Bina and Sonu and the rest of the children had followed their teachers into the school playground. Feeling a little lost, Bina looked around for Prakash. She found herself facing a dark slender young woman wearing spectacles, who must have been in her early twenties—just a little too old to be another student. She had a kind, expressive face and she seemed a little concerned by all that had been happening.

Bina noticed that she had lovely hands; it was obvious that the new teacher hadn't milked cows or worked in the fields!

'You must be new here,' said the teacher, smiling at Bina. 'And is this your little brother?'

'Yes, we've come from Koli village. We were at school there.'

'It's a long walk from Koli. You didn't see any leopards, did you? Well, I'm new too. Are you in the sixth class?'

'Sonu is in the third. I'm in the sixth.'

'Then I'm your new teacher. My name is Tania Ramola. Come along, let's see if we can settle down in our classroom.'

■

Mr Mani turned up at twelve o'clock, wondering what all the fuss was about. No, he snapped, he had not been attacked by a leopard; and yes, he had lost his pyjamas and would someone kindly return them to him?

'How did you lose your pyjamas, sir?' asked Prakash.

'They were blown off the washing line!' snapped Mr Mani.

After much questioning, Mr Mani admitted that he had gone further than he had intended, and that he had lost his way coming back. He had been a bit upset because the new teacher, a slip of a girl, had been given charge of the sixth, while he was still with the fifth, along with that troublesome boy Prakash, who kept on reminding him of the time! The headmaster had explained that as Mr Mani was due to retire at the end of the year, the school did not wish to burden him with a senior class. But Mr Mani looked upon the whole thing as a plot to get rid of him. He glowered at Miss Ramola whenever he passed her. And when she smiled back at him, he looked the other way!

Mr Mani had been getting even more absent-minded of late—putting on his shoes without his socks, wearing his homespun waistcoat inside out, mixing up people's names and, of course, eating other people's lunches and dinners. His sister had made a mutton broth for the postmaster, who was down with 'flu' and had asked Mr Mani to take it over in a thermos. When the postmaster opened the thermos, he found only a few drops of broth at the bottom—Mr Mani had drunk the rest somewhere along the way.

When sometimes Mr Mani spoke of his coming retirement, it was to describe his plans for the small field he owned just behind the house. Right now, it was full of potatoes, which did not require much looking after; but he had plans for growing dahlias, roses, French beans, and other fruits and flowers.

The next time he visited Tehri, he promised himself, he would buy some dahlia bulbs and rose cuttings. The monsoon season would be a good time to put them down. And meanwhile, his potatoes were still flourishing.

3

Bina enjoyed her first day at the new school. She felt at ease with Miss Ramola, as did most of the boys and girls in her class. Tania Ramola had been to distant towns such as Delhi and Lucknow—places they had only heard about—and it was said that she had a brother who was a pilot and flew planes all over the world. Perhaps he'd fly over Nauti some day!

Most of the children had of course seen planes flying overhead, but none of them had seen a ship, and only a few had been in a train. Tehri mountain was far from the railway and hundreds of miles from the sea. But they all knew about the big dam that was being built at Tehri, just forty miles away.

Bina, Sonu and Prakash had company for part of the way home, but gradually the other children went off in different directions. Once they had crossed the stream, they were on their own again.

It was a steep climb all the way back to their village. Prakash had a supply of peanuts which he shared with Bina and Sonu, and at a small spring they quenched their thirst.

When they were less than a mile from home, they met a postman who had finished his round of the villages in the area and was now returning to Nauti.

'Don't waste time along the way,' he told them. 'Try to get home before dark.'

'What's the hurry?' asked Prakash, glancing at his watch. 'It's only five o'clock.'

'There's a leopard around. I saw it this morning, not far from the stream. No one is sure how it got here. So don't take any chances. Get home early.'

'So there really is a leopard,' said Sonu.

They took his advice and walked faster, and Sonu forgot to complain about his aching feet.

They were home well before sunset.

There was a smell of cooking in the air and they were hungry.

'Cabbage and roti,' said Prakash gloomily. 'But I could eat anything today.' He stopped outside his small slate-roofed house, and Bina and Sonu waved goodbye and carried on across a couple of ploughed fields until they reached their small stone house.

'Stuffed tomatoes,' said Sonu, sniffing just outside the front door.

'And lemon pickle,' said Bina, who had helped cut, sun and salt the lemons a month previously.

Their mother was lighting the kitchen stove. They greeted her with great hugs and demands for an immediate dinner. She was a good cook who could make even the simplest of dishes taste delicious. Her favourite saying was, 'Home-made bread is better than roast meat abroad,' and Bina and Sonu had to agree.

Electricity had yet to reach their village, and they took their meal by the light of a kerosene lamp. After the meal, Sonu settled down to do a little homework, while Bina stepped outside to look at the stars.

Across the fields, someone was playing a flute. 'It must be Prakash,' thought Bina. 'He always breaks off on the high notes.' But the flute music was simple and appealing, and she began singing softly to herself in the dark.

4

Mr Mani was having trouble with the porcupines. They had been getting into his garden at night and digging up and eating his potatoes. From his bedroom window—left open, now that the mild April weather had arrived—he could listen to them enjoying the vegetables he had worked hard to grow. Scrunch, scrunch! Katar, katar, as their sharp teeth sliced through the largest and juiciest of potatoes. For Mr Mani it was as though they were biting through his own flesh. And the sound of them digging industriously as they rooted up those healthy, leafy plants made him tremble with rage and indignation. The unfairness of it all!

Yes, Mr Mani hated porcupines. He prayed for their destruction, their removal from the face of the earth. But, as his friends were quick to point out, 'The creator made porcupines too,' and in any case you could never see the creatures or catch them, they were completely nocturnal.

Mr Mani got out of bed every night, torch in one hand,

a stout stick in the other but, as soon as he stepped into the garden, the crunching and digging stopped and he was greeted by the most infuriating of silences. He would grope around in the dark, swinging wildly with the stick, but not a single porcupine was to be seen or heard. As soon as he was back in bed, the sounds would start all over again—scrunch, scrunch, katar, katar...

Mr Mani came to his class tired and dishevelled, with rings beneath his eyes and a permanent frown on his face. It took some time for his pupils to discover the reason for his misery, but when they did, they felt sorry for their teacher and took to discussing ways and means of saving his potatoes from the porcupines.

It was Prakash who came up with the idea of a moat or water ditch. 'Porcupines don't like water,' he said knowledgeably.

'How do you know?' asked one of his friends.

'Throw water on one and see how it runs! They don't like getting their quills wet.'

There was no one who could disprove Prakash's theory, and the class fell in with the idea of building a moat, especially as it meant getting most of the day off.

'Anything to make Mr Mani happy,' said the Headmaster, and the rest of the school watched with envy as the pupils of Class 5, armed with spades and shovels collected from all parts of the village, took up their positions around Mr Mani's potato field and began digging a ditch.

By evening the moat was ready, but it was still dry and the porcupines got in again that night and had a great feast.

'At this rate,' said Mr Mani gloomily, 'there won't be any potatoes left to save.'

But the next day, Prakash and the other boys and girls managed to divert the water from a stream that flowed past the village. They had the satisfaction of watching it flow gently into the ditch. Everyone went home in a good mood. By nightfall, the ditch had overflowed, the potato field was flooded, and Mr Mani found himself trapped inside his house. But Prakash and his friends had won the day. The porcupines stayed away that night!

■

A month had passed, and wild violets, daisies and buttercups now sprinkled the hill slopes and, on her way to school, Bina gathered enough to make a little posy. The bunch of flowers fitted easily into an old ink well. Miss Ramola was delighted to find this little display in the middle of her desk.

'Who put these here?' she asked in surprise.

Bina kept quiet, and the rest of the class smiled secretively. After that, they took turns bringing flowers for the classroom.

On her long walks to school and home again, Bina became aware that April was the month of new leaves. The oak leaves were bright green above and silver beneath, and when they rippled in the breeze they were clouds of silvery green. The path was strewn with old leaves, dry and crackly. Sonu loved kicking them around.

Clouds of white butterflies floated across the stream. Sonu was chasing a butterfly when he stumbled over something dark and repulsive. He went sprawling on the grass. When he got to his feet, he looked down at the remains of a small animal.

'Bina! Prakash! Come quickly!' he shouted.

It was part of a sheep, killed some days earlier by a much larger animal.

'Only a leopard could have done this,' said Prakash.

'Let's get away, then,' said Sonu. 'It might still be around!'

'No, there's nothing left to eat. The leopard will be hunting elsewhere by now. Perhaps it's moved on to the next valley.'

'Still, I'm frightened,' said Sonu. 'There may be more leopards!'

Bina took him by the hand. 'Leopards don't attack humans!' she said.

'They will, if they get a taste for people!' insisted Prakash.

'Well, this one hasn't attacked any people as yet,' said Bina, although she couldn't be sure. Hadn't there been rumours of a leopard attacking some workers near the dam? But she did not want Sonu to feel afraid, so she did not mention the story. All she said was, 'It has probably come here because of all the activity near the dam.'

All the same, they hurried home. And for a few days, whenever they reached the stream, they crossed over very quickly, unwilling to linger too long at that lovely spot.

5

A few days later, a school party was on its way to Tehri to see the new dam that was being built.

Miss Ramola had arranged to take her class, and Mr Mani, not wishing to be left out, insisted on taking his class as well. That meant there were about fifty boys and girls taking part in the outing. The little bus could only take thirty. A friendly truck driver agreed to take some children if they were prepared to sit on sacks of potatoes. And Prakash persuaded the owner of the diesel-roller to turn it round and head it back to Tehri—with him and a couple of friends up on the driving seat.

Prakash's small group set off at sunrise, as they had to walk some distance in order to reach the stranded road roller. The bus left at 9 a.m. with Miss Ramola and her class, and Mr Mani and some of his pupils. The truck was to follow later.

It was Bina's first visit to a large town, and her first bus ride.

The sharp curves along the winding, downhill road made several children feel sick. The bus driver seemed to be in a tearing hurry. He took them along at a rolling, rollicking speed, which made Bina feel quite giddy. She rested her head on her arms and refused to look out of the window. Hairpin bends and cliff edges, pine forests and snowcapped peaks, all swept past her, but she felt too ill to want to look at anything. It was just as well—those sudden drops, hundreds of feet to the valley below, were quite frightening. Bina began to wish that she hadn't come—or that she had joined Prakash on the road roller instead!

Miss Ramola and Mr Mani didn't seem to notice the lurching and groaning of the old bus. They had made this journey many times. They were busy arguing about the advantages and disadvantages of large dams—an argument that was to continue on and off for much of the day.

Meanwhile, Prakash and his friends had reached the roller. The driver hadn't turned up, but they managed to reverse it and get it going in the direction of Tehri. They were soon overtaken by both bus and truck but kept moving along at a steady chug. Prakash spotted Bina at the window of the bus and waved cheerfully. She responded feebly.

Bina felt better when the road levelled out near Tehri. As they crossed an old bridge over the wide river, they were startled by a loud bang which made the bus shudder. A cloud of dust rose above the town.

'They're blasting the mountain,' said Miss Ramola.

'End of a mountain,' said Mr Mani, mournfully.

While they were drinking cups of tea at the bus stop, waiting for the potato truck and the road roller, Miss Ramola and Mr Mani continued their argument about the dam. Miss Ramola maintained that it would bring electric power and water for irrigation to large areas of the country, including the surrounding area. Mr Mani declared that it was a menace, as it was situated in an earthquake zone. There would be a terrible disaster if the dam burst! Bina found it all very confusing. And what about the animals in the area, she wondered, what would happen to them?

The argument was becoming quite heated when the potato truck arrived. There was no sign of the road roller, so it was decided that Mr Mani should wait for Prakash and his friends while Miss Ramola's group went ahead.

•

Some eight or nine miles before Tehri, the road roller had broken down, and Prakash and his friends were forced to walk. They had not gone far, however, when a mule train came along—five or six mules that had been delivering sacks of grain in Nauti. A boy rode on the first mule, but the others had no loads.

'Can you give us a ride to Tehri?' called Prakash.

'Make yourselves comfortable,' said the boy.

There were no saddles, only gunny sacks strapped on to the mules with rope. They had a rough but jolly ride down to the Tehri bus stop. None of them had ever ridden mules; but they had saved at least an hour on the road.

Looking around the bus stop for the rest of the party, they could find no one from their school. And Mr Mani, who should have been waiting for them, had vanished.

6

Tania Ramola and her group had taken the steep road to the hill above Tehri. Half an hour's climbing brought them to a little plateau which overlooked the town, the river and the dam site.

The earthworks for the dam were only just coming up, but a wide tunnel had been bored through the mountain to divert the river into another channel. Down below, the old town was still spread out across the valley and from a distance it looked quite charming and picturesque.

'Will the whole town be swallowed up by the waters of the dam?' asked Bina.

'Yes, all of it,' said Miss Ramola. 'The clock tower and the old palace. The long bazaar, and the temples, the schools and the jail, and hundreds of houses, for many miles up the valley. All those people will have to go—thousands of them! Of course they'll be resettled elsewhere.'

'But the town's been here for hundreds of years,' said Bina. 'They were quite happy without the dam, weren't they?'

'I suppose they were. But the dam isn't just for them—it's for the millions who live further downstream, across the plains.'

'And it doesn't matter what happens to this place?'

'The local people will be given new homes, somewhere else.' Miss Ramola found herself on the defensive and decided to change the subject. 'Everyone must be hungry. It's time we had our lunch.'

Bina kept quiet. She didn't think the local people would want to go away. And it was a good thing, she mused, that there was only a small stream and not a big river running past her village. To be uprooted like this—a town and hundreds of villages—and put down somewhere on the hot, dusty plains—seemed to her unbearable.

'Well, I'm glad I don't live in Tehri,' she said.

She did not know it, but all the animals and most of the birds had already left the area. The leopard had been among them.

∎

They walked through the colourful, crowded bazaar, where fruit sellers did business beside silversmiths, and pavement vendors sold everything from umbrellas to glass bangles. Sparrows attacked sacks of grain, monkeys made off with bananas, and stray cows and dogs rummaged in refuse bins, but nobody took any notice. Music blared from radios. Buses blew their horns. Sonu bought a whistle to add to the general din, but Miss Ramola told him to put it away. Bina had kept five rupees aside, and now she used it to buy a cotton headscarf for her mother.

As they were about to enter a small restaurant for a meal, they were joined by Prakash and his companions; but of Mr Mani there was still no sign.

'He must have met one of his relatives,' said Prakash. 'He has relatives everywhere.'

After a simple meal of rice and lentils, they walked the length of the bazaar without seeing Mr Mani. At last, when they were about to give up the search, they saw him emerge from a by-lane, a large sack slung over his shoulder.

'Sir, where have you been?' asked Prakash. 'We have been looking for you everywhere.'

On Mr Mani's face was a look of triumph.

'Help me with this bag,' he said breathlessly.

'You've bought more potatoes, sir,' said Prakash.

'Not potatoes, boy. Dahlia bulbs!'

7

It was dark by the time they were all back in Nauti. Mr Mani had refused to be separated from his sack of dahlia bulbs, and had been forced to sit in the back of the truck with Prakash and most of the boys.

Bina did not feel so ill on the return journey. Going uphill was definitely better than going downhill! But by the time the bus reached Nauti it was too late for most of the children to walk back to the more distant villages. The boys were put up in different homes, while the girls were given beds in the school veranda.

The night was warm and still. Large moths fluttered around the single bulb that lit the veranda. Counting moths, Sonu soon fell asleep. But Bina stayed awake for some time, listening to the sounds of the night. A nightjar went tonk-tonk in the bushes, and somewhere in the forest an owl hooted softly. The sharp call of a barking deer travelled up the valley, from the direction of the stream. Jackals kept howling. It seemed that there were more of them than ever before.

Bina was not the only one to hear the barking deer. The leopard, stretched full length on a rocky ledge, heard it too. The leopard raised its head and then got up slowly. The deer was its natural prey. But there weren't many left, and that was why the leopard, robbed of its forest by the dam, had taken to attacking dogs and cattle near the villages.

As the cry of the barking deer sounded nearer, the leopard left its lookout point and moved swiftly through the shadows towards the stream.

8

In early June the hills were dry and dusty, and forest fires broke out, destroying shrubs and trees, killing birds and small animals. The resin in the pines made these trees burn more fiercely, and the wind would take sparks from the trees and carry them into the dry grass and leaves, so that new fires would spring up before the old ones had died out. Fortunately, Bina's village was not in the pine belt; the fires did not reach it. But Nauti was surrounded by a fire that raged for three days, and the children had to stay away from school.

And then, towards the end of June, the monsoon rains arrived and there was an end to forest fires. The monsoon lasts three months and the lower Himalayas would be drenched in rain, mist and cloud for the next three months.

The first rain arrived while Bina, Prakash and Sonu were returning home from school. Those first few drops on the dusty path made them cry out with excitement. Then the rain grew heavier and a wonderful aroma rose from the earth.

'The best smell in the world!' exclaimed Bina.

Everything suddenly came to life. The grass, the crops, the trees, the birds. Even the leaves of the trees glistened and looked new.

That first wet weekend, Bina and Sonu helped their mother plant beans, maize and cucumbers. Sometimes, when the rain was very heavy, they had to run indoors. Otherwise they worked in the rain, the soft mud clinging to their bare legs.

Prakash now owned a dog, a black dog with one ear up and one ear down. The dog ran around getting in everyone's way, barking at cows, goats, hens and humans, without frightening any of them. Prakash said it was a very clever dog, but no one else seemed to think so. Prakash also said it would protect the village from the leopard, but others said the dog would be the first to be taken—he'd run straight into the jaws of Mr Spots!

In Nauti, Tania Ramola was trying to find a dry spot in the quarters she'd been given. It was an old building and the roof was leaking in several places. Mugs and buckets were scattered about the floor in order to catch the drips.

Mr Mani had dug up all his potatoes and presented them to the friends and neighbours who had given him lunches and dinners. He was having the time of his life, planting dahlia bulbs all over his garden.

'I'll have a field of many-coloured dahlias!' he announced. 'Just wait till the end of August!'

'Watch out for those porcupines,' warned his sister. 'They eat dahlia bulbs too!'

Mr Mani made an inspection tour of his moat, no longer in flood, and found everything in good order. Prakash had done his job well.

■

Now, when the children crossed the stream, they found that the water level had risen by about a foot. Small cascades had turned into waterfalls. Ferns had sprung up on the banks. Frogs chanted.

Prakash and his dog dashed across the stream. Bina and Sonu followed more cautiously. The current was much stronger now and the water was almost up to their knees. Once they had crossed the stream, they hurried along the path, anxious not to be caught in a sudden downpour.

By the time they reached school, each of them had two or three leeches clinging to their legs. They had to use salt to remove them. The leeches were the most troublesome part of the rainy season. Even the leopard did not like them. It could not lie in the long grass without getting leeches on its paws and face.

One day, when Bina, Prakash and Sonu were about to cross the stream they heard a low rumble, which grew louder every second. Looking up at the opposite hill, they saw several trees shudder, tilt outwards and begin to fall. Earth and rocks bulged out from the mountain, then came crashing down into the ravine.

'Landslide!' shouted Sonu.

'It's carried away the path,' said Bina. 'Don't go any further.'

There was a tremendous roar as more rocks, trees and bushes fell away and crashed down the hillside.

Prakash's dog, who had gone ahead, came running back, tail between his legs.

They remained rooted to the spot until the rocks had stopped falling and the dust had settled. Birds circled the area, calling wildly. A frightened barking deer ran past them.

'We can't go to school now,' said Prakash. 'There's no way around.'

They turned and trudged home through the gathering mist.

In Koli, Prakash's parents had heard the roar of the landslide. They were setting out in search of the children when they saw them emerge from the mist, waving cheerfully.

9

They had to miss school for another three days, and Bina was afraid they might not be able to take their final exams. Although Prakash was not really troubled at the thought of missing exams, he did not like feeling helpless just because their path had been swept away. So he explored the hillside until he found a goat-track going around the mountain. It joined up with another path near Nauti. This made their walk longer by a mile, but Bina did not mind. It was much cooler now that the rains were in full swing.

The only trouble with the new route was that it passed close to the leopard's lair. The animal had made this area its own since being forced to leave the dam area.

One day Prakash's dog ran ahead of them, barking furiously. Then he ran back, whimpering.

'He's always running away from something,' observed Sonu. But a minute later he understood the reason for the dog's fear.

They rounded a bend and Sonu saw the leopard standing in their way. They were struck dumb—too terrified to run. It was a strong, sinewy creature. A low growl rose from its throat. It seemed ready to spring.

They stood perfectly still, afraid to move or say a word. And the leopard must have been equally surprised. It stared at them for a few seconds, then bounded across the path and into the oak forest.

Sonu was shaking. Bina could hear her heart hammering. Prakash could only stammer: 'Did you see the way he sprang? Wasn't he beautiful?'

He forgot to look at his watch for the rest of the day.

A few days later, Sonu stopped and pointed to a large outcrop of rock on the next hill.

The leopard stood far above them, outlined against the sky. It looked strong, majestic. Standing beside it were two young cubs.

'Look at those little ones!' exclaimed Sonu.

'So it's a female, not a male,' said Prakash.

'That's why she was killing so often,' said Bina. 'She had to feed her cubs too.'

They remained still for several minutes, gazing up at the leopard and her cubs. The leopard family took no notice of them.

'She knows we are here,' said Prakash, 'but she doesn't care. She knows we won't harm them.'

'We are cubs too!' said Sonu.

'Yes,' said Bina. 'And there's still plenty of space for all of us. Even when the dam is ready there will still be room for leopards and humans.'

10

The school exams were over. The rains were nearly over too. The landslide had been cleared, and Bina, Prakash and Sonu were once again crossing the stream.

There was a chill in the air, for it was the end of September.

Prakash had learnt to play the flute quite well, and he played on the way to school and then again on the way home. As a result he did not look at his watch so often.

One morning they found a small crowd in front of Mr Mani's house.

'What could have happened?' wondered Bina. 'I hope he hasn't got lost again.'

'Maybe he's sick,' said Sonu.

'Maybe it's the porcupines,' said Prakash.

But it was none of these things.

Mr Mani's first dahlia was in bloom, and half the village had turned up to look at it! It was a huge red double dahlia, so heavy that it had to be supported with sticks. No one had ever seen such a magnificent flower!

Mr Mani was a happy man. And his mood only improved over the coming week, as more and more dahlias flowered— crimson, yellow, purple, mauve, white—button dahlias, pom-pom dahlias, spotted dahlias, striped dahlias...Mr Mani had them all! A dahlia even turned up on Tania Romola's desk—he got along quite well with her now—and another brightened up the Headmaster's study.

A week later, on their way home—it was almost the last day of the school term—Bina, Prakash and Sonu talked about what they might do when they grew up.

'I think I'll become a teacher,' said Bina. 'I'll teach children about animals and birds, and trees and flowers.'

'Better than maths!' said Prakash.

'I'll be a pilot,' said Sonu. 'I want to fly a plane like Miss Ramola's brother.'

'And what about you, Prakash?' asked Bina.

Prakash just smiled and said, 'Maybe I'll be a flute player,' and he put the flute to his lips and played a sweet melody.

'Well, the world needs flute players too,' said Bina, as they fell into step beside him.

The leopard had been stalking a barking deer. She paused when she heard the flute and the voices of the children. Her own young ones were growing quickly, but the girl and the two boys did not look much older.

They had started singing their favourite song again.

'Five more miles to go!
We climb through rain and snow,
A river to cross...
A mountain to pass...
Now we've four more miles to go!'

The leopard waited until they had passed, before returning to the trail of the barking deer.

♪

A Case for Inspector Lal

I MET Inspector Keemat Lal about two years ago, while I was living in the hot, dusty town of Shahpur in the plains of northern India.

Keemat Lal had charge of the local police station. He was a heavily built man, slow and rather ponderous, and inclined to be lazy; but, like most lazy people, he was intelligent. He was also a failure. He had remained an inspector for a number of years, and had given up all hope of further promotion. His luck was against him, he said. He should never have been a policeman. He had been born under the sign of Capricorn and should really have gone into the restaurant business, but now it was too late to do anything about it.

The inspector and I had little in common. He was nearing forty, and I was twenty-five. But both of us spoke English, and in Shahpur there were very few people who did. In addition, we were both fond of beer. There were no places of entertainment in Shahpur. The searing heat, the dust that came whirling up from the east, the mosquitoes (almost as numerous as the flies) and the general monotony gave one a thirst for something more substantial than stale lemonade.

My house was on the outskirts of the town, where we were not often disturbed. On two or three evenings in the week, just as the sun was going down and making it possible for one to emerge from the khas-cooled confines of a dark, high-ceilinged bedroom, Inspector Keemat Lal would appear on the veranda steps, mopping the sweat from his face with a small towel, which he used instead of a handkerchief. My only servant, excited at the prospect of serving an inspector of police, would hurry out with glasses, a bucket of ice and several bottles of the best Indian beer.

One evening, after we had overtaken our fourth bottle, I said, 'You must have had some interesting cases in your career, Inspector.'

'Most of them were rather dull,' he said. 'At least the successful ones were. The sensational cases usually went unsolved—otherwise I might have been a superintendent by now. I suppose you are talking of murder cases. Do you remember the shooting of the minister of the interior? I was on that one, but it was a political murder and we never solved it.'

'Tell me about a case you solved,' I said. 'An interesting one.' When I saw him looking uncomfortable, I added, 'You don't have to worry, Inspector. I'm a very discreet person, in spite of all the beer I consume.'

'But how can you be discreet? You are a writer.'

I protested: 'Writers are usually very discreet. They always change the names of people and places.'

He gave me one of his rare smiles. 'And how would you describe me, if you were to put me into a story?'

'Oh, I'd leave you as you are. No one would believe in you, anyway.'

He laughed indulgently and poured out more beer. 'I suppose I can change names, too... I will tell you of a very interesting case. The victim was an unusual person, and so was the killer. But you must promise not to write this story.'

'I promise,' I lied.

'Do you know Panauli?'

'In the hills? Yes, I have been there once or twice.'

'Good, then you will follow me without my having to be too descriptive. This happened about three years ago, shortly after I had been stationed at Panauli. Nothing much ever happened there. There were a few cases of theft and cheating, and an occasional fight during the summer. A murder took place about once every ten years. It was therefore quite an event when the Rani of—was found dead in her sitting room, her head split open with an axe. I knew that I would have to solve the case if I wanted to stay in Panauli.

'The trouble was, anyone could have killed the rani, and there were some who made no secret of their satisfaction that she was dead. She had been an unpopular woman. Her husband was dead, her children were scattered, and her money—for she had never been a very wealthy rani—had been dwindling away. She lived alone in an old house on the outskirts of the town, ruling the locality with the stern authority of a matriarch. She had a servant, and he was the man who found the body and came to the police, dithering and tongue-tied. I arrested him at once, of course. I knew he was probably innocent, but a basic rule is to grab the first man on the scene of crime, especially if he happens to be a servant. But we let him go after a beating. There was nothing much he could tell us, and he had a sound alibi.

'The axe with which the rani had been killed must have been a small woodcutter's axe—so we deduced from the wound. We couldn't find the weapon. It might have been used by a man or a woman, and there were several of both sexes who had a grudge against the rani. There were bazaar rumours that she had been supplementing her income by trafficking in young women: she had the necessary connections. There were also rumours that she possessed vast wealth, and that it was stored away in her godowns. We did not find any treasure. There were so many rumours darting about like battered shuttlecocks that

I decided to stop wasting my time in trying to follow them up. Instead, I restricted my inquiries to those people who had been close to the rani—either in their personal relationships or in actual physical proximity.

'To begin with, there was Mr Kapur, a wealthy businessman from Bombay who had a house in Panauli. He was supposed to be an old admirer of the rani's. I discovered that he had occasionally lent her money, and that, in spite of his professed friendship for her, had charged a high rate of interest.

'Then there were her immediate neighbours—an American missionary and his wife, who had been trying to convert the rani to Christianity; an English spinster of seventy, who made no secret of the fact that she and the rani had hated each other with great enthusiasm; a local councillor and his family, who did not get on well with their aristocratic neighbour; and a tailor, who kept his shop close by. None of these people had any powerful motive for killing the rani—or none that I could discover. But the tailor's daughter interested me.

'Her name was Kusum. She was twelve or thirteen years old—a thin, dark girl, with lovely black eyes and a swift, disarming smile. While I was making my routine inquiries in the vicinity of the rani's house, I noticed that the girl always tried to avoid me. When I questioned her about the rani, and about her own movements on the day of the crime, she pretended to be very vague and stupid.

'But I could see she was not stupid, and I became convinced that she knew something unusual about the rani. She might even know something about the murder. She could have been protecting someone, and was afraid to tell me what she knew. Often, when I spoke to her of the violence of the rani's death, I saw fear in her eyes. I began to think the girl's life might be in danger, and I had a close watch kept on her. I liked her. I liked her youth and freshness, and the innocence and wonder in her eyes. I spoke to her whenever I could, kindly and paternally, and though I knew she rather liked me and found me amusing—the ups and downs of Panauli always left me panting for breath—and though I could see that she *wanted* to tell me something, she always held back at the last moment.

'Then, one afternoon, while I was in the rani's house going through her effects, I saw something glistening in a narrow crack near the doorstep. I would not have noticed it if the sun had not been pouring through the window, glinting off the little object. I stooped and picked up a piece of glass. It was part of a broken bangle.

'I turned the fragment over in my hand. There was something familiar about its colour and design. Didn't Kusum wear similar glass bangles? I went to look for the girl but she was not in her father's shop. I was told that she had gone down the hill, to gather firewood.

'I decided to take the narrow path down the hill. It went round some rocks and cacti, and then disappeared into a forest of oak trees. I found Kusum sitting at the edge of the forest, a bundle of twigs beside her.

'"You are always wandering about alone," I said. "Don't you feel afraid?"

'"It is safer when I am alone," she replied. "Nobody comes here."

'I glanced quickly at the bangles on her wrist, and noticed that their colour matched that of the broken piece. I held out the bit of broken glass and said, "I found it in the rani's house. It must have fallen..."

'She did not wait for me to finish what I was saying. With a look of terror, she sprang up from the grass and fled into the forest.

'I was completely taken aback. I had not expected such a reaction. Of what significance was the broken bangle? I hurried after the girl, slipping on the smooth pine needles that covered the slopes. I was searching amongst the trees when I heard someone sobbing behind me. When I turned round, I saw the girl standing on a boulder, facing me with an axe in her hands.

'When Kusum saw me staring at her, she raised the axe and rushed down the slope towards me.

'I was too bewildered to be able to do anything but stare with open mouth as she rushed at me with the axe. The impetus of her run would have brought her right up against me, and the axe, coming down, would probably have crushed my skull, thick though it is. But while she was still six feet from me, the axe flew out of her hands. It sprang into the air as though it had a life of its own and came curving towards me.

'In spite of my weight, I moved swiftly aside. The axe grazed my shoulder and sank into the soft bark of the tree behind me. And Kusum dropped at my feet weeping hysterically.'

Inspector Keemat Lal paused in order to replenish his glass. He took a long pull at the beer, and the froth glistened on his moustache.

'And then what happened?' I prompted him.

'Perhaps it could only have happened in India—and to a person like me,' he said. 'This sudden compassion for the person you are supposed to destroy. Instead of being furious and outraged, instead of seizing the girl and marching her off to the police station, I stroked her head and said silly comforting things.'

'And she told you that she had killed the rani?'

'She told me how the rani had called her to her house and given her tea and sweets. Mr Kapur had been there. After some time he began stroking Kusum's arms and squeezing her knees.

She had drawn away, but Kapur kept pawing her. The rani was telling Kusum not to be afraid, that no harm would come to her. Kusum slipped away from the man and made a rush for the door. The rani caught her by the shoulders and pushed her back into the room. The rani was getting angry. Kusum saw the axe lying in a corner of the room. She seized it, raised it above her head and threatened Kapur. The man realized that he had gone too far, and valuing his neck, backed away. But the rani, in a great rage, sprang at the girl. And Kusum, in desperation and panic, brought the axe down upon the rani's head.

'The rani fell to the ground. Without waiting to see what Kapur might do, Kusum fled from the house. Her bangle must have broken when she stumbled against the door. She ran into the forest, and after concealing the axe amongst some tall ferns, lay weeping on the grass until it grew dark. But such was her nature, and such the resilience of youth, that she recovered sufficiently to be able to return home looking her normal self. And during the following days, she managed to remain silent about the whole business.'

'What did you do about it?' I asked.

Keemat Lal looked me straight in my beery eye.

'Nothing,' he said. 'I did absolutely nothing. I couldn't have the girl put away in a remand home. It would have crushed her spirit.'

'And what about Kapur?'

'Oh, he had his own reasons for remaining quiet, as you may guess. No, the case was closed—or perhaps I should say the file was put in my pending tray. My promotion, too, went into the pending tray.'

'It didn't turn out very well for you,' I said.

'No. Here I am in Shahpur, and still an inspector. But, tell me, what would you have done if you had been in my place?'

I considered his question carefully for a moment or two, then said, 'I suppose it would have depended on how much sympathy the girl evoked in me. She had killed in innocence...'

'Then, you would have put your personal feeling above your duty to uphold the law?'

'Yes. But I would not have made a very good policeman.'

'Exactly.'

'Still, it's a pity that Kapur got off so easily.'

'There was no alternative if I was to let the girl go. But he didn't get off altogether. He found himself in trouble later on for swindling some manufacturing concern, and went to jail for a couple of years.'

'And the girl—did you see her again?'

'Well, before I was transferred from Panauli, I saw her occasionally on the road. She was usually on her way to school. She would greet me with folded hands, and call me uncle.'

The beer bottles were all empty, and Inspector Keemat Lal got up to leave. His final words to me were, 'I should never have been a policeman.'

✗

The Thief's Story

I was still a thief when I met Romi. And though I was only fifteen years old, I was an experienced and fairly successful hand. Romi was watching a wrestling match when I approached him. He was about twenty-five and he looked easy-going, kind, and simple enough for my purpose. I was sure I would be able to win the young man's confidence.

'You look a bit of a wrestler yourself,' I said. There's nothing like flattery to break the ice!

'So do you,' he replied, which put me off for a moment because at that time I was rather thin and bony.

'Well,' I said modestly, 'I do wrestle a bit.'

'What's your name?'

'Hari Singh,' I lied. I took a new name every month, which kept me ahead of the police and former employers.

After these formalities Romi confined himself to commenting on the wrestlers, who were grunting, gasping and heaving each other about. When he walked away, I followed him casually.

'Hello again,' he said.

I gave him my most appealing smile. 'I want to work for you,' I said.

'But I can't pay you anything—not for some time, anyway.'

I thought that over for a minute. Perhaps I had misjudged my man. 'Can you feed me?' I asked.

'Can you cook?'

'I can cook,' I lied again.

'If you can cook, then maybe I can feed you.'

He took me to his room over the Delhi Sweet Shop and told me I could sleep on the balcony. But the meal I cooked that night must have been terrible because Romi gave it to a stray dog and told me to be off.

But I just hung around, smiling in my most appealing way, and he couldn't help laughing.

Later, he said never mind, he'd teach me to cook. He also taught me to write my name and said he would soon teach me to write whole sentences and to add figures. I was grateful. I knew that once I could write like an educated person, there would be no limit to what I could achieve.

It was quite pleasant working for Romi. I made tea in the morning and then took my time buying the day's supplies, usually making a profit of two or three rupees. I think he knew I made a little money this way, but he didn't seem to mind.

Romi made money by fits and starts. He would borrow one week, lend the next. He kept worrying about his next cheque, but as soon as it arrived he would go out and celebrate. He wrote for the *Delhi* and *Bombay* magazines: a strange way to make a living.

One evening he came home with a small bundle of notes, saying he had just sold a book to a publisher. That night I saw him put the money in an envelope and tuck it under the mattress.

I had been working for Romi for almost a month and, apart from cheating on the shopping, had not done anything big in my real line of work. I had every opportunity for doing so. I could come and go as I pleased, and Romi was the most trusting person I had ever met.

That was why it was so difficult to rob him. It was easy for me to rob a greedy man. But robbing a nice man could be a problem. And if he doesn't notice he's being robbed, then all the spice goes out of the undertaking!

Well, it's time I got down to some real work, I told myself. If I don't take the money, he'll only waste it on his so-called friends. After all, he doesn't even give me a salary.

Romi was sleeping peacefully. A beam of moonlight reached over the balcony and fell on his bed. I sat on the floor, considering the situation. If I took the money, I could catch the 10.30 express to Lucknow. Slipping out of my blanket, I crept over to the bed.

My hand slid under the mattress, searching for the notes. When I found the packet, I drew it out without a sound. Romi sighed in his sleep and turned on his side. Startled, I moved quickly out of the room.

Once on the road, I began to run. I had the money stuffed into a vest pocket under my shirt. When I'd gotten some distance from Romi's place, I slowed to a walk and, taking the envelope from my pocket, counted the money. Seven hundred rupees in fifties. I could live like a prince for a week or two!

When I reached the station, I did not stop at the ticket office (I had never bought a ticket in my life) but dashed straight on to the platform. The Lucknow Express was just moving out. The train had still to pick up speed and I should have been able to jump into one of the compartments, but I hesitated—for some reason I can't explain—and I lost the chance to get away.

When the train had gone, I found myself standing alone on the deserted platform. I had no idea where to spend the night. I had no friends, believing that friends were more trouble than help. And I did not want to arouse curiosity by staying at one of the small hotels nearby. The only person I knew really well was the man I had robbed. Leaving the station, I walked slowly through the bazaar.

In my short career, I had made a study of people's faces after they had discovered the loss of their valuables. The greedy showed panic; the rich showed anger; the poor, resignation. But I knew that Romi's face when he discovered the theft would show only a touch of sadness—not for the loss of money, but for the loss of trust.

The night was chilly—November nights can be cold in northern India—and a shower of rain added to my discomfort. I sat down in the shelter of the clock tower. A few beggars and vagrants lay beside me, rolled up tight in their blankets. The clock showed midnight. I felt for the notes; they were soaked through.

Romi's money. In the morning, he would probably have given me five rupees to go to the movies, but now I had it all: no more cooking meals, running to the bazaar, or learning to write sentences.

Sentences! I had forgotten about them in the excitement of the theft. Writing complete sentences, I knew, could one day bring me more than a few hundred rupees. It was a simple matter to steal. But to be a really big man, a clever and respected man, was something else. I should go back to Romi, I told myself, if only to learn to read and write.

I hurried back to the room feeling very nervous, for it is much easier to steal something than to return it undetected.

I opened the door quietly, then stood in the doorway in clouded moonlight. Romi was still asleep. I crept to the head of the bed, and my hand came up with the packet of notes. I felt his breath on my hand. I remained still for a few moments. Then my fingers found the edge of the mattress, and I slipped the money beneath it.

I awoke late the next morning to find that Romi had already made the tea. He stretched out a hand to me. There was a fifty-rupee note between his fingers. My heart sank.

'I made some money yesterday,' he said. 'Now I'll be able to pay you regularly.'

My spirits rose. But when I took the note, I noticed that it was still wet from the night's rain.

So he knew what I'd done. But neither his lips nor his eyes revealed anything.

'Today we'll start writing sentences,' he said.

I smiled at Romi in my most appealing way. And the smile came by itself, without any effort.

✦

The Trouble with Jinns

My friend Jimmy has only one arm. He lost the other when he was a young man of twenty-five. The story of how he lost his good right arm is a little difficult to believe, but I swear that it is absolutely true.

To begin with, Jimmy was (and presumably still is) a Jinn. Now a Jinn isn't really a human like us. A Jinn is a spirit creature from another world who has assumed, for a lifetime, the physical aspect of a human being. Jimmy was a true Jinn and he had the Jinn's gift of being able to elongate his arm at will. Most Jinns can stretch their arms to a distance of twenty or thirty feet. Jimmy could attain forty feet. His arm would move through space or up walls or along the ground like a beautiful gliding serpent. I have seen him stretched out beneath a mango tree, helping himself to ripe mangoes from the top of the tree. He loved mangoes. He was a natural glutton and it was probably his gluttony that first led him to misuse his peculiar gifts.

We were at school together at a hill station in northern India. Jimmy was particularly good at basketball. He was clever enough not to lengthen his arm too much because he did not want anyone to know that he was a Jinn. In the boxing ring he generally won his fights. His opponents never seemed to get past his amazing reach. He just kept tapping them on the nose until they retired from the ring bloody and bewildered.

It was during the half-term examinations that I stumbled on Jimmy's secret. We had been set a particularly difficult algebra paper but I had managed to cover a couple of sheets with correct answers and was about to forge ahead on another sheet when I noticed someone's hand on my desk. At first I thought it was the invigilator's. But when I looked up there was no one beside me.

Could it be the boy sitting directly behind? No, he was engrossed in his question paper and had his hands to himself. Meanwhile, the hand on my desk had grasped my answer sheets and was cautiously moving off. Following its descent, I found that it was attached to an arm of amazing length and pliability. This moved stealthily down the desk and slithered across the floor, shrinking all the while, until it was restored to its normal length. Its owner was of course one who had never been any good at algebra.

I had to write out my answers a second time but after the exam I went straight up to Jimmy, told him I didn't like his game and threatened to expose him. He begged me not to let anyone know, assured me that he couldn't really help himself, and offered to be of service to me whenever I wished. It was tempting to have Jimmy as my friend, for with his long reach he would obviously be useful. I agreed to overlook the matter of the pilfered papers and we became the best of pals.

It did not take me long to discover that Jimmy's gift was more of a nuisance than a constructive aid. That was because Jimmy had a second-rate mind and did not know how to make proper use of his powers. He seldom rose above the trivial. He used his long arm in the tuck shop, in the classroom, in the dormitory. And when we were allowed out to the cinema, he used it in the dark of the hall.

Now the trouble with all Jinns is that they have a weakness for women with long black hair. The longer and blacker the hair, the better for Jinns. And should a Jinn manage to take possession of the woman he desires, she goes into a decline and her beauty decays. Everything about her is destroyed except for the beautiful long black hair.

Jimmy was still too young to be able to take possession in this way, but he couldn't resist touching and stroking long black hair. The cinema was the best place for the indulgence of his whims. His arm would start stretching, his fingers would feel their way along the rows of seats, and his lengthening limb would slowly work its way along the aisle until it reached the back of the seat in which sat the object of his admiration. His hand would stroke the long black hair with great tenderness and if the girl felt anything and looked round, Jimmy's hand would disappear behind the seat and lie there poised like the hood of a snake, ready to strike again.

At college two or three years later, Jimmy's first real victim succumbed to his attentions. She was a lecturer in economics, not very good looking, but her hair, black and lustrous, reached almost to her knees. She usually kept it in plaits but Jimmy saw her one morning just after she had taken a head bath, and her hair lay spread out on the cot on which she was reclining. Jimmy could no longer control himself. His spirit, the very essence of his personality, entered the woman's body and the next day she was distraught, feverish and excited. She would not eat, went into a coma, and in a few days dwindled to a mere skeleton. When she died, she was nothing but skin and bone but her hair had lost none of its loveliness.

I took pains to avoid Jimmy after this tragic event. I could not prove that he was the cause of the lady's sad demise but in my own heart I was quite certain of it. For since meeting Jimmy, I had read a good deal about Jinns and knew their ways.

We did not see each other for a few years. And then, holidaying in the hills last year, I found we were staying at the same hotel. I could not very well ignore him and after we had drunk a few beers together I began to feel that I had perhaps misjudged Jimmy and that he was not the irresponsible Jinn I had taken him for. Perhaps the college lecturer had died of some mysterious malady that attacks only college lecturers and Jimmy had nothing at all to do with it.

We had decided to take our lunch and a few bottles of beer to a grassy knoll just below the main motor road. It was late afternoon and I had been sleeping off the effects of the beer when I woke to find Jimmy looking rather agitated.

'What's wrong?' I asked.

'Up there, under the pine trees,' he said. 'Just above the road. Don't you see them?'

'I see two girls,' I said. 'So what?'

'The one on the left. Haven't you noticed her hair?'

'Yes, it is very long and beautiful and—now look, Jimmy, you'd better get a grip on yourself!' But already his hand was out of sight, his arm snaking up the hillside and across the road.

Presently I saw the hand emerge from some bushes near the girls and then cautiously make its way to the girl with the black tresses. So absorbed was Jimmy in the pursuit of his favourite pastime that he failed to hear the blowing of a horn. Around the bend of the road came a speeding Mercedes Benz truck.

Jimmy saw the truck but there wasn't time for him to shrink his arm back to normal. It lay right across the entire width of the road and when the truck had passed over it, it writhed and twisted like a mortally wounded python.

By the time the truck driver and I could fetch a doctor, the arm (or what was left of it) had shrunk to its ordinary size. We took Jimmy to hospital where the doctors found it necessary to amputate. The truck driver, who kept insisting that the arm he ran over was at least thirty feet long, was arrested on a charge of drunken driving.

Some weeks later I asked Jimmy, 'Why are you so depressed? You still have one arm. Isn't it gifted in the same way?'

'I never tried to find out,' he said, 'and I'm not going to try now.'

He is, of course, still a Jinn at heart and whenever he sees a girl with long black hair he must be terribly tempted to try out his one good arm and stroke her beautiful tresses. But he has learnt his lesson. It is better to be a human without any gifts than a Jinn or a genius with one too many.

ʃ

Adventures in Reading

1

You don't see them so often now, those tiny books and almanacs—genuine pocket books—once so popular with our parents and grandparents; much smaller than the average paperback, often smaller than the palm of the hand. With the advent of coffee-table books, new books keep growing bigger and bigger, rivalling tombstones! And one day, like Alice after drinking from the wrong bottle, they will reach the ceiling and won't have anywhere else to go. The average publisher, who apparently believes that large profits are linked to large books, must look upon these old miniatures with amusement or scorn. They were not meant for a coffee table, true. They were meant for true book lovers and readers, for they took up very little space—you could slip them into your pocket without any discomfort, either to you or to the pocket.

I have a small collection of these little books, treasured over the years. Foremost is my father's prayer book and psalter, with his name, 'Aubrey Bond, Lovedale, 1917', inscribed on the inside back cover. Lovedale is a school in the Nilgiri Hills in South India, where, as a young man, he did his teacher's training. He gave it to me soon after I went to a boarding school in Shimla in 1944, and my own name is inscribed on it in his beautiful handwriting.

Another beautiful little prayer book in my collection is called *The Finger Prayer Book*. Bound in soft leather, it is about the same length and breadth as the average middle finger. Replete with psalms, it is the complete book of common prayer and not an abridgement; a marvel of miniature book production.

Not much larger is a delicate item in calf leather, *The Humour of Charles Lamb*. It fits into my wallet and often stays there. It has a tiny portrait of the great essayist, followed by some thirty to forty extracts from his essays, such as this favourite of mine: 'Every dead man must take upon himself to be lecturing me with his odious truism, that "Such as he is now, I must shortly be". Not so shortly friend, perhaps as thou imaginest. In the meantime, I am alive. I move about. I am worth twenty of thee. Know thy betters!'

No fatalist, Lamb. He made no compromise with Father Time. He affirmed that in age we must be as glowing and tempestuous as in youth! And yet Lamb is thought to be an old-fashioned writer.

Another favourite among my 'little' books is *The Pocket Trivet, An Anthology for Optimists*, published by *The Morning Post* newspaper in 1932. But what is a trivet, the unenlightened may well ask. Well, it's a stand for a small pot or kettle, fixed securely over a grate. To be right as a trivet is to be perfectly right. Just right, like the short sayings in this book, which is further enlivened by a number of charming woodcuts based on the seventeenth century originals; such as the illustration of a moth hovering over a candle flame and below it the legend—'I seeke mine owne hurt.'

But the sayings are mostly of a cheering nature, such as Emerson's 'Hitch your wagon to a star!' or the West Indian proverb: 'Every day no Christmas, an' every day no rainy day.'

My book of trivets is a happy example of much concentrated

wisdom being collected in a small space—the beauty separated from the dross. It helps me to forget the dilapidated building in which I live and to look instead at the ever-changing cloud patterns as seen from my bedroom windows. There is no end to the shapes made by the clouds, or to the stories they set off in my head. We don't have to circle the world in order to find beauty and fulfilment. After all, most of living has to happen in the mind. And, to quote one anonymous sage from my trivet, 'The world is only the size of each man's head.'

2

Amongst the current fraternity of writers, I must be that very rare person—an author who actually writes by hand!

Soon after the invention of the typewriter, most editors and publishers understandably refused to look at any mansucript that was handwritten. A decade or two earlier, when Dickens and Balzac had submitted their hefty manuscrips in longhand, no one had raised any objection. Had their handwriting been awful, their manuscripts would still have been read. Fortunately for all concerned, most writers, famous or obscure, took pains over their handwriting. For some, it was an art in itself, and many of those early manuscripts are a pleasure to look at and read.

And it wasn't only authors who wrote with an elegant hand. Parents and grandparents of most of us had distinctive styles of their own. I still have my father's last letter, written to me when I was at boarding school in Shimla some fifty years ago. He used large, beautifully formed letters, and his thoughts seemed to have the same flow and clarity as his handwriting.

In his letter he advises me (then a nine-year-old) about my own handwriting: 'I wanted to write before about your writing, Ruskin... Sometimes I get letters from you in very small writing, as if you wanted to squeeze everything into one sheet of letter paper. It is not good for you or for your eyes, to get into the habit of writing too small... Try and form a larger style of handwriting—use more paper if necessary!'

I did my best to follow his advice, and I'm glad to report that after nearly forty years of the writing life, most people can still read my handwriting!

Word processors are all the rage now, and I have no objection to these mechanical aids any more than I have to my old Olympia typewriter, made in 1956 and still going strong. Although I do all my writing in longhand, I follow the conventions by typing a second draft. But I would not enjoy my writing if I had to do it straight on to a machine. It isn't just the pleasure of writing longhand. I like taking my notebooks and writing pads to odd places. This particular essay is being written on the steps of my small cottage facing Pari Tibba (Fairy Hill). Part of the reason for sitting here is that there is a new postman on this route, and I don't want him to miss me.

For a freelance writer, the postman is almost as important as a publisher. I could, of course, sit here doing nothing, but as I have pencil and paper with me, and feel like using them, I shall write until the postman comes and maybe after he has gone, too! There is really no way in which I could set up a word processor on these steps.

There are a number of favourite places where I do my writing. One is under the chestnut tree on the slope above the cottage. Word processors were not designed keeping mountain slopes in mind. But armed with a pen (or pencil) and paper, I can lie on the grass and write for hours. On one occasion, last month, I did take my typewriter into the garden, and I am still trying to extricate an acorn from under the keys, while the roller seems permanently stained yellow with some fine pollen dust from the deodar trees.

My friends keep telling me about all the wonderful things I can do with a word processor, but they haven't got around to finding me one that I can take to bed, for that is another place where I do much of my writing—especially on cold winter nights, when it is impossible to keep the cottage warm.

While the wind howls outside, and snow piles up on the windowsill, I am warm under my quilt, writing pad on my knees, ballpoint pen at the ready. And if, next day, the weather is warm and sunny, these simple aids will accompany me on a long walk, ready for instant use should I wish to record an incident, a prospect, a conversation or simply a train of thought.

When I think of the great eighteenth- and nineteenth-century writers, scratching away with their quill pens, filling hundreds of pages every month, I am amazed to find that their handwriting did not deteriorate into the sort of hieroglyphics that often make up the average doctor's prescription today. They knew they had to write legibly, if only for the sake of the typesetters.

Both Dickens and Thackeray had good, clear, flourishing styles. (Thackeray was a clever illustrator, too.) Somerset Maugham had an upright, legible hand. Churchill's neat handwriting never wavered, even when he was under stress. I like the bold, clear, straighforward hand of Abraham Lincoln; it mirrors the man. Mahatma Gandhi, another great soul who fell to the assassin's bullet, had many similarities of both handwriting and outlook.

Not everyone had a beautiful hand. King Henry VIII had an untidy scrawl, but then, he was not a man of much refinement. Guy Fawkes, who tried to blow up the British Parliament, had a very shaky hand. With such a quiver, no wonder he failed in his attempt! Hitler's signature is ugly, as you would expect. And Napoleon's doesn't seem to know where to stop; how much like the man!

I think my father was right when he said handwriting was often the key to a man's character, and that large, well-formed letters went with an uncluttered mind. Florence Nightingale had a lovely handwriting, the hand of a caring person. And there were many like her amongst our forebears.

3

When I was a small boy, no Christmas was really complete unless my Christmas stocking contained several recent issues of my favourite comic paper. If today my friends complain that I am too voracious a reader of books, they have only these comics to blame; for they were the origin, if not of my tastes in reading, then certainly of the reading habit itself.

I like to think that my conversion to comics began at the age of five, with a comic strip on the children's page of *The Statesman*. In the late 1930s, Benji, whose head later appeared only on the Benji League badge, had a strip to himself; I don't remember his adventures very clearly, but every day (or was it once a week?) I would cut out the Benji strip and paste it into a scrapbook. Two years later, this scrapbook, bursting with the adventures of Benji, accompanied me to boarding school, where, of course, it passed through several hands before finally passing into limbo.

Of course, comics did not form the only reading matter that found its way into my Christmas stocking. Before I was eight, I had read *Peter Pan, Alice,* and most of *Mr Midshipman Easy*; but I had also consumed thousands of comic papers which were, after all, slim affairs and mostly pictorial, 'certain little penny books radiant with gold and rich with bad pictures', as Leigh Hunt described the children's papers of his own time.

But though they were mostly pictorial, comics in those

days did have a fair amount of reading matter, too. *The Hostspur, Wizard, Magnet* (a victim of the Second World War) and *Champion* contained stories woven round certain popular characters. In *Champion*, which I read regularly right through my prep school years, there was Rockfist Rogan, Royal Air Force (RAF), a pugilist who managed to combine boxing with bombing, and Fireworks Flynn, a footballer who always scored the winning goal in the last two minutes of play.

Billy Bunter has, of course, become one of the immortals—almost a subject for literary and social historians. Quite recently, *The Times Literary Supplement* devoted its first two pages to an analysis of the Bunter stories. Eminent lawyers and doctors still look back nostalgically to the arrival of the weekly *Magnet;* they are now the principal customers for the special souvenir edition of the first issue of the *Magnet*, recently reprinted in facsimile. Bunter, 'forever young', has become a folk hero. He is seen on stage, screen and television, and is even quoted in the House of Commons.

From this, I take courage. My only regret is that I did not preserve my own early comics—not because of any bibliophilic value which they might possess today, but because of my sentimental regard for early influences in art and literature.

The first venture in children's publishing, in 1774, was a comic of sorts. In that year, John Newberry brought out:

According to Act of Parliament (neatly bound and gilt):
A Little Pretty Pocket-Book, intended for the Instruction and Amusement of Little Master Tommy and Pretty Miss Polly, with an agreeable Letter to read from Jack the Giant-Killer...

The book contained pictures, rhymes and games. Newberry's characters and imaginary authors included Woglog the Giant,

Tommy Trip, Giles Gingerbread, Nurse Truelove, Peregrine Puzzlebrains, Primrose Prettyface and many others with names similar to those found in the comic papers of our own century.

Newberry was also the originator of the 'Amazing Free Offer', so much a part of American comics. At the beginning of 1755, he had this to offer:

> Nurse Truelove's New Year Gift, or the Book of Books for children, adorned with Cuts and designed as a Present for every little boy who would become a great Man and ride upon a fine Horse; and to every little Girl who would become a great Woman and ride in a Lord Mayor's gilt Coach. Printed for the Author, who has ordered these books to be given gratis to all little Boys in St. Paul's churchyard, they paying for the Binding, which is only Two pence each Book.

Many of today's comics are crude and, like many television serials, violent in their appeal. But I did not know American comics until I was twelve, and by then I had become quite discriminating. Superman, Bulletman, Batman and Green Lantern, and other super heroes all left me cold. I had, by then, passed into the world of real books but the weakness for the comic strip remains. I no longer receive comics in my Christmas stocking, but I do place a few in the stockings of Gautam and Siddharth. And, needless to say, I read them right through beforehand.

✗

The Blue Umbrella

1

'Neelu! Neelu!' cried Binya.

She scrambled barefoot over the rocks, ran over the short summer grass, up and over the brow of the hill, all the time calling 'Neelu, Neelu!'

Neelu—Blue—was the name of the blue-grey cow. The other cow, which was white, was called Gori, meaning Fair One. They were fond of wandering off on their own, down to the stream or into the pine forest, and sometimes they came back by themselves and sometimes they stayed away—almost deliberately, it seemed to Binya.

If the cows didn't come home at the right time, Binya would be sent to fetch them. Sometimes her brother, Bijju, went with her, but these days he was busy preparing for his exams and didn't have time to help with the cows.

Binya liked being on her own, and sometimes she allowed the cows to lead her into some distant valley, and then they would all be late coming home. The cows preferred having Binya with them, because she let them wander. Bijju pulled them by their tails if they went too far.

Binya belonged to the mountains, to this part of the Himalayas known as Garhwal. Dark forests and lonely hilltops held no terrors for her. It was only when she was in the market town, jostled by the crowds in the bazaar, that she felt rather nervous and lost. The town, five miles from the village, was also a pleasure resort for tourists from all over India.

Binya was probably ten. She may have been nine or even eleven, she couldn't be sure because no one in the village kept birthdays; but her mother told her she'd been born during a winter when the snow had come up to the windows, and that was just over ten years ago, wasn't it? Two years later, her father had died, but his passing had made no difference to their way of life. They had three tiny terraced fields on the side of the mountain, and they grew potatoes, onions, ginger, beans, mustard and maize: not enough to sell in the town, but enough to live on.

Like most mountain girls, Binya was quite sturdy, fair of skin, with pink cheeks and dark eyes and her black hair tied in a pigtail. She wore pretty glass bangles on her wrists, and a necklace of glass beads. From the necklace hung a leopard's claw. It was a lucky charm, and Binya always wore it. Bijju had one, too, only his was attached to a string.

Binya's full name was Binyadevi, and Bijju's real name was Vijay, but everyone called them Binya and Bijju. Binya was two years younger than her brother.

She had stopped calling for Neelu; she had heard the cowbells tinkling, and knew the cows hadn't gone far. Singing to herself, she walked over fallen pine needles into the forest glade on the spur of the hill. She heard voices, laughter, the clatter of plates and cups, and stepping through the trees, she came upon a party of picnickers.

They were holiday-makers from the plains. The women were dressed in bright saris, the men wore light summer shirts, and the children had pretty new clothes. Binya, standing in the shadows between the trees, went unnoticed; for some time she watched the picnickers, admiring their clothes, listening to their unfamiliar accents, and gazing rather hungrily at the sight of all their food. And then her gaze came to rest on a bright blue umbrella, a frilly thing for women, which lay open on the grass beside its owner.

Now Binya had seen umbrellas before, and her mother had a big black umbrella which nobody used any more because the field rats had eaten holes in it, but this was the first time Binya had seen such a small, dainty, colourful umbrella and she fell in love with it. The umbrella was like a flower, a great blue flower that had sprung up on the dry brown hillside.

She moved forward a few paces so that she could see the umbrella better. As she came out of the shadows into the sunlight, the picnickers saw her.

'Hello, look who's here!' exclaimed the older of the two women. 'A little village girl!'

'Isn't she pretty?' remarked the other. 'But how torn and dirty her clothes are!' It did not seem to bother them that Binya could hear and understand everything they said about her.

'They're very poor in the hills,' said one of the men.

'Then let's give her something to eat.' And the older woman beckoned to Binya to come closer.

Hesitantly, nervously, Binya approached the group. Normally she would have turned and fled, but the attraction was the pretty blue umbrella. It had cast a spell over her, drawing her forward almost against her will.

'What's that on her neck?' asked the younger woman.

'A necklace of sorts.'

'It's a pendant—see, there's a claw hanging from it!'

'It's a tiger's claw,' said the man beside her. (He had never seen a tiger's claw.) 'A lucky charm. These people wear them to keep away evil spirits.' He looked to Binya for confirmation, but Binya said nothing.

'Oh, I want one too!' said the woman, who was obviously his wife.

'You can't get them in shops.'

'Buy hers, then. Give her two or three rupees, she's sure to need the money.'

The man, looking slightly embarrassed but anxious to please his young wife, produced a two-rupee note and offered it to Binya, indicating that he wanted the pendant in exchange. Binya put her hand to the necklace, half afraid that the excited woman would snatch it away from her. Solemnly she shook her head. The man then showed her a five-rupee note, but again Binya shook her head.

'How silly she is!' exclaimed the young woman.

'It may not be hers to sell,' said the man. 'But I'll try again. How much do you want—what can we give you?' And he waved his hand towards the picnic things scattered about on the grass.

Without any hesitation Binya pointed to the umbrella.

'My umbrella!' exclaimed the young woman. 'She wants my umbrella. What cheek!'

'Well, you want her pendant, don't you?'

'That's different.'

'Is it?'

The man and his wife were beginning to quarrel with each other.

'I'll ask her to go away,' said the older woman. 'We're making such fools of ourselves.'

'But I want the pendant!' cried the other, petulantly. And then, on an impulse, she picked up the umbrella and held it out to Binya. 'Here, take the umbrella!'

Binya removed her necklace and held it out to the young woman, who immediately placed it around her own neck. Then Binya took the umbrella and held it up. It did not look so small in her hands; in fact, it was just the right size.

She had forgotten about the picnickers, who were busy examining the pendant. She turned the blue umbrella this way and that, looked through the bright blue silk at the pulsating sun, and then, still keeping it open, turned and disappeared into the forest glade.

2

Binya seldom closed the blue umbrella. Even when she had it in the house, she left it lying open in a corner of the room. Sometimes Bijju snapped it shut, complaining that it got in the way. She would open it again a little later. It wasn't beautiful when it was closed.

Whenever Binya went out—whether it was to graze the cows, or fetch water from the spring, or carry milk to the little tea shop on the Tehri road—she took the umbrella with her. That patch of sky-blue silk could always be seen on the hillside.

Old Ram Bharosa (Ram the Trustworthy) kept the tea shop on the Tehri road. It was a dusty, unmetalled road. Once a day, the Tehri bus stopped near his shop and passengers got down to sip hot tea or drink a glass of curd. He kept a few bottles of Coca-Cola too, but as there was no ice, the bottles got hot in the sun and so were seldom opened. He also kept sweets and toffees, and when Binya or Bijju had a few coins to spare, they would spend them at the shop. It was only a mile from the village.

Ram Bharosa was astonished to see Binya's blue umbrella. 'What have you there, Binya?' he asked.

Binya gave the umbrella a twirl and smiled at Ram Bharosa. She was always ready with her smile, and would willingly have lent it to anyone who was feeling unhappy.

'That's a lady's umbrella,' said Ram Bharosa. 'That's only for memsahibs. Where did you get it?'

'Someone gave it to me—for my necklace.'

'You exchanged it for your lucky claw!'

Binya nodded.

'But what do you need it for? The sun isn't hot enough, and it isn't meant for the rain. It's just a pretty thing for rich ladies to play with!'

Binya nodded and smiled again. Ram Bharosa was quite right; it was just a beautiful plaything. And that was exactly why she had fallen in love with it.

'I have an idea,' said the shopkeeper. 'It's no use to you, that umbrella. Why not sell it to me? I'll give you five rupees for it.'

'It's worth fifteen,' said Binya.

'Well, then, I'll give you ten.'

Binya laughed and shook her head.

'Twelve rupees?' said Ram Bharosa, but without much hope.

Binya placed a five-paise coin on the counter. 'I came for a toffee,' she said.

Ram Bharosa pulled at his drooping whiskers, gave Binya a wry look, and placed a toffee in the palm of her hand. He watched Binya as she walked away along the dusty road. The blue umbrella held him fascinated, and he stared after it until it was out of sight.

The villagers used this road to go to the market town. Some used the bus, a few rode on mules and most people walked. Today, everyone on the road turned their heads to stare at the girl with the bright blue umbrella.

Binya sat down in the shade of a pine tree. The umbrella, still open, lay beside her. She cradled her head in her arms, and presently she dozed off. It was that kind of day, sleepily warm and summery.

And while she slept, a wind sprang up.

It came quietly, swishing gently through the trees, humming softly. Then it was joined by other random gusts, bustling over the tops of the mountains. The trees shook their heads and came to life. The wind fanned Binya's cheeks. The umbrella stirred on the grass.

The wind grew stronger, picking up dead leaves and sending them spinning and swirling through the air. It got into the umbrella and began to drag it over the grass. Suddenly it lifted the umbrella and carried it about six feet from the sleeping girl. The sound woke Binya.

She was on her feet immediately, and then she was leaping down the steep slope. But just as she was within reach of the umbrella, the wind picked it up again and carried it further downhill.

Binya set off in pursuit. The wind was in a wicked, playful mood. It would leave the umbrella alone for a few moments but as soon as Binya came near, it would pick up the umbrella again and send it bouncing, floating, dancing away from her.

The hill grew steeper. Binya knew that after twenty yards it would fall away in a precipice. She ran faster. And the wind ran with her, ahead of her, and the blue umbrella stayed up with the wind.

A fresh gust picked it up and carried it to the very edge of the cliff. There it balanced for a few seconds, before toppling over, out of sight.

Binya ran to the edge of the cliff. Going down on her hands and knees, she peered down the cliff face. About a hundred feet below, a small stream rushed between great boulders. Hardly anything grew on the cliff face—just a few stunted bushes, and, halfway down, a wild cherry tree growing crookedly out of the rocks and hanging across the chasm. The umbrella had stuck in the cherry tree.

Binya didn't hesitate. She may have been timid with strangers, but she was at home on a hillside. She stuck her bare leg over the edge of the cliff and began climbing down. She kept her face to the hillside, feeling her way with her feet, only changing her handhold when she knew her feet were secure. Sometimes she held on to the thorny bilberry bushes, but she did not trust the other plants which came away very easily.

Loose stones rattled down the cliff. Once on their way, the stones did not stop until they reached the bottom of the hill; and they took other stones with them, so that there was soon a cascade of stones, and Binya had to be very careful not to start a landslide.

As agile as a mountain goat, she did not take more than five minutes to reach the crooked cherry tree. But the most difficult task remained—she had to crawl along the trunk of the tree, which stood out at right angles from the cliff. Only by doing this could she reach the trapped umbrella.

Binya felt no fear when climbing trees. She was proud of the fact that she could climb them as well as Bijju. Gripping the rough cherry bark with her toes, and using her knees as leverage, she crawled along the trunk of the projecting tree until she was almost within reach of the umbrella. She noticed with dismay that the blue cloth was torn in a couple of places.

She looked down, and it was only then that she felt afraid. She was right over the chasm, balanced precariously about eighty feet above the boulder-strewn stream. Looking down, she felt quite dizzy. Her hands shook, and the tree shook too. If she slipped now, there was only one direction in which she could fall—down, down, into the depths of that dark and shadowy ravine.

There was only one thing to do; concentrate on the patch

of blue just a couple of feet away from her.

She did not look down or up, but straight ahead, and willing herself forward, she managed to reach the umbrella.

She could not crawl back with it in her hands. So, after dislodging it from the forked branch in which it had stuck, she let it fall, still open, into the ravine below. Cushioned by the wind, the umbrella floated serenely downwards, landing in a thicket of nettles.

Binya crawled back along the trunk of the cherry tree.

Twenty minutes later, she emerged from the nettle clump, her precious umbrella held aloft. She had nettle stings all over her legs, but she was hardly aware of the smarting. She was as immune to nettles as Bijju was to bees.

3

About four years previously, Bijju had knocked a hive out of an oak tree, and had been badly stung on the face and legs. It had been a painful experience. But now, if a bee stung him, he felt nothing at all: he had been immunized for life!

He was on his way home from school. It was two o'clock and he hadn't eaten since six in the morning. Fortunately, the Kingora bushes—the bilberries—were in fruit, and already Bijju's lips were stained purple with the juice of the wild, sour fruit.

He didn't have any money to spend at Ram Bharosa's shop, but he stopped there anyway to look at the sweets in their glass jars.

'And what will you have today?' asked Ram Bharosa.

'No money,' said Bijju.

'You can pay me later.'

Bijju shook his head. Some of his friends had taken sweets on credit, and at the end of the month they had found they'd eaten more sweets than they could possibly pay for! As a result, they'd had to hand over to Ram Bharosa some of their most treasured possessions—such as a curved knife for cutting grass, or a small hand-axe, or a jar for pickles, or a pair of earrings—and these had become the shopkeeper's possessions and were kept by him or sold in his shop.

Ram Bharosa had set his heart on having Binya's blue umbrella, and so naturally he was anxious to give credit to either of the children, but so far neither had fallen into the trap.

Bijju moved on, his mouth full of Kingora berries. Halfway home, he saw Binya with the cows. It was late evening, and the sun had gone down, but Binya still had the umbrella open. The two small rents had been stitched up by her mother.

Bijju gave his sister a handful of berries. She handed him the umbrella while she ate the berries.

'You can have the umbrella until we get home,' she said. It was her way of rewarding Bijju for bringing her the wild fruit.

Calling 'Neelu! Gori!' Binya and Bijju set out for home, followed at some distance by the cows.

It was dark before they reached the village, but Bijju still had the umbrella open.

■

Most of the people in the village were a little envious of Binya's blue umbrella. No one else had ever possessed one like it. The schoolmaster's wife thought it was quite wrong for a poor cultivator's daughter to have such a fine umbrella while she, a second-class B.A., had to make do with an ordinary black one. Her husband offered to have their old umbrella dyed blue; she gave him a scornful look, and loved him a little less than before. The pujari, who looked after the temple, announced that he would buy a multicoloured umbrella the next time he was in the town. A few days later he returned looking annoyed and grumbling that they weren't available except in Delhi. Most people consoled themselves by saying that Binya's pretty umbrella wouldn't keep out the rain, if it rained heavily; that it would shrivel in the sun, if the sun was fierce; that it would collapse in a wind, if the wind was strong; that it would attract lightning, if lightning fell near it; and that it would prove unlucky, if there was any ill luck going about. Secretly, everyone admired it.

Unlike the adults, the children didn't have to pretend. They were full of praise for the umbrella. It was so light, so pretty, so bright a blue! And it was just the right size for Binya. They knew that if they said nice things about the umbrella, Binya would smile and give it to them to hold for a little while—just a very little while!

Soon it was the time of the monsoon. Big black clouds kept piling up, and thunder rolled over the hills.

Binya sat on the hillside all afternoon, waiting for the rain. As soon as the first big drop of rain came down, she raised the umbrella over her head. More drops, big ones, came pattering down. She could see them through the umbrella silk, as they broke against the cloth.

And then there was a cloudburst, and it was like standing under a waterfall. The umbrella wasn't really a rain umbrella, but it held up bravely. Only Binya's feet got wet. Rods of rain fell around her in a curtain of shivered glass.

Everywhere on the hillside people were scurrying for shelter. Some made for a charcoal burner's hut, others for a mule-shed, or Ram Bharosa's shop. Binya was the only one who didn't run. This was what she'd been waiting for—rain on her umbrella—and she wasn't in a hurry to go home. She didn't mind getting her feet wet. The cows didn't mind getting wet either.

Presently she found Bijju sheltering in a cave. He would

have enjoyed getting wet, but he had his school books with him and he couldn't afford to let them get spoilt. When he saw Binya, he came out of the cave and shared the umbrella. He was a head taller than his sister, so he had to hold the umbrella for her, while she held his books.

The cows had been left far behind.

'Neelu, Neelu!' called Binya.

'Gori!' called Bijju.

When their mother saw them sauntering home through the driving rain, she called out: 'Binya! Bijju! Hurry up and bring the cows in! What are you doing out there in the rain?'

'Just testing the umbrella,' said Bijju.

4

The rains set in, and the sun only made brief appearances. The hills turned a lush green. Ferns sprang up on walls and tree trunks. Giant lilies reared up like leopards from the tall grass. A white mist coiled and uncoiled as it floated up from the valley. It was a beautiful season, except for the leeches.

Every day, Binya came home with a couple of leeches fastened to the flesh of her bare legs. They fell off by themselves just as soon as they'd had their thimbleful of blood, but you didn't know they were on you until they fell off, and then, later, the skin became very sore and itchy. Some of the older people still believed that to be bled by leeches was a remedy for various ailments. Whenever Ram Bharosa had a headache, he applied a leech to his throbbing temple.

Three days of incessant rain had flooded out a number of small animals who lived in holes in the ground. Binya's mother suddenly found the roof full of field rats. She had to drive them out; they ate too much of her stored-up wheat flour and rice.

Bijju liked lifting up large rocks to disturb the scorpions who were sleeping beneath. And snakes came out to bask in the sun.

Binya had just crossed the small stream at the bottom of the hill when she saw something gliding out of the bushes and coming towards her. It was a long black snake. A clatter of loose stones frightened it. Seeing the girl in its way, it rose up, hissing, prepared to strike. The forked tongue darted out, the venomous head lunged at Binya.

Binya's umbrella was open as usual. She thrust it forward, between herself and the snake, and the snake's hard snout thudded twice against the strong silk of the umbrella. The reptile then turned and slithered away over the wet rocks, disappearing into a clump of ferns.

Binya forgot about the cows and ran all the way home to tell her mother how she had been saved by the umbrella. Bijju had to put away his books and go out to fetch the cows. He carried a stout stick, in case he met with any snakes.

■

First the summer sun, and now the endless rain, meant that the umbrella was beginning to fade a little. From a bright blue it had changed to a light blue. But it was still a pretty thing, and tougher than it looked, and Ram Bharosa still desired it. He did not want to sell it; he wanted to own it. He was probably the richest man in the area—so why shouldn't he have a blue umbrella? Not a day passed without his getting a glimpse of Binya and the umbrella; and the more he saw the umbrella, the more he wanted it.

The schools closed during the monsoon, but this didn't mean that Bijju could sit at home doing nothing. Neelu and Gori were providing more milk than was required at home, so Binya's mother was able to sell a kilo of milk every day: half a kilo to the schoolmaster, and half a kilo (at reduced rate) to the temple pujari. Bijju had to deliver the milk every morning.

Ram Bharosa had asked Bijju to work in his shop during the holidays, but Bijju didn't have time—he had to help his mother with the ploughing and the transplanting of the rice seedlings. So Ram Bharosa employed a boy from the next village, a boy called Rajaram. He did all the washing-up, and ran various errands. He went to the same school as Bijju, but the two boys were not friends.

One day, as Binya passed the shop, twirling her blue umbrella, Rajaram noticed that his employer gave a deep sigh and began muttering to himself.

'What's the matter, Babuji?' asked the boy.

'Oh, nothing,' said Ram Bharosa. 'It's just a sickness that has come upon me. And it's all due to that girl Binya and her wretched umbrella.'

'Why, what has she done to you?'

'Refused to sell me her umbrella! There's pride for you. And I offered her ten rupees.'

'Perhaps, if you gave her twelve...'

'But it isn't new any longer. It isn't worth eight rupees now. All the same, I'd like to have it.'

'You wouldn't make a profit on it,' said Rajaram.

'It's not the profit I'm after, wretch! It's the thing itself. It's the beauty of it!'

'And what would you do with it, Babuji? You don't visit anyone—you're seldom out of your shop. Of what use would it be to you?'

'Of what use is a poppy in a cornfield? Of what use is a rainbow? Of what use are you, numbskull? Wretch! I, too, have a soul. I want the umbrella, because—because I want its beauty to be mine!'

Rajaram put the kettle on to boil, began dusting the counter, all the time muttering: 'I'm as useful as an umbrella,' and then, after a short period of intense thought, said: 'What will you give me, Babuji, if I get the umbrella for you?'

'What do you mean?' asked the old man.

'You know what I mean. What will you give me?'

'You mean to steal it, don't you, you wretch? What a delightful child you are! I'm glad you're not my son or my enemy. But look, everyone will know it has been stolen, and then how will I be able to show off with it?'

'You will have to gaze upon it in secret,' said Rajaram with a chuckle. 'Or take it into Tehri, and have it coloured red! That's your problem. But tell me, Babuji, do you want it badly enough to pay me three rupees for stealing it without being seen?'

Ram Bharosa gave the boy a long, sad look. 'You're a sharp boy,' he said. 'You'll come to a bad end. I'll give you two rupees.'

'Three,' said the boy.

'Two,' said the old man.

'You don't really want it, I can see that,' said the boy.

'Wretch!' said the old man. 'Evil one! Darkener of my doorstep! Fetch me the umbrella, and I'll give you three rupees.'

5

Binya was in the forest glade where she had first seen the umbrella. No one came there for picnics during the monsoon. The grass was always wet and the pine needles were slippery underfoot. The tall trees shut out the light, and poisonous-looking mushrooms, orange and purple, sprang up everywhere. But it was a good place for porcupines, who seemed to like the mushrooms, and Binya was searching for porcupine quills.

The hill people didn't think much of porcupine quills, but

far away in southern India, the quills were valued as charms and sold at a rupee each. So Ram Bharosa paid a tenth of a rupee for each quill brought to him, and he in turn sold the quills at a profit to a trader from the plains.

Binya had already found five quills, and she knew there'd be more in the long grass. For once, she'd put her umbrella down. She had to put it aside if she was to search the ground thoroughly.

It was Rajaram's chance.

He'd been following Binya for some time, concealing himself behind trees and rocks, creeping closer whenever she became absorbed in her search. He was anxious that she should not see him and be able to recognize him later.

He waited until Binya had wandered some distance from the umbrella. Then, running forward at a crouch, he seized the open umbrella and dashed off with it.

But Rajaram had very big feet. Binya heard his heavy footsteps and turned just in time to see him as he disappeared between the trees. She cried out, dropped the porcupine quills, and gave chase.

Binya was swift and sure-footed, but Rajaram had a long stride. All the same, he made the mistake of running downhill. A long-legged person is much faster going uphill than down. Binya reached the edge of the forest glade in time to see the thief scrambling down the path to the stream. He had closed the umbrella so that it would not hinder his flight.

Binya was beginning to gain on the boy. He kept to the path, while she simply slid and leapt down the steep hillside. Near the bottom of the hill the path began to straighten out, and it was here that the long-legged boy began to forge ahead again.

Bijju was coming home from another direction. He had a bundle of sticks which he'd collected for the kitchen fire. As he reached the path, he saw Binya rushing down the hill as though all the mountain spirits in Garhwal were after her.

'What's wrong?' he called. 'Why are you running?'

Binya paused only to point at the fleeing Rajaram.

'My umbrella!' she cried. 'He has stolen it!'

Bijju dropped his bundle of sticks, and ran after his sister. When he reached her side, he said, 'I'll soon catch him!' and went sprinting away over the lush green grass. He was fresh, and he was soon well ahead of Binya and gaining on the thief.

Rajaram was crossing the shallow stream when Bijju caught up with him. Rajaram was the taller boy, but Bijju was much stronger. He flung himself at the thief, caught him by the legs, and brought him down in the water. Rajaram got to his feet and tried to drag himself away, but Bijju still had him by a leg. Rajaram overbalanced and came down with a great splash. He had let the umbrella fall. It began to float away on the current. Just then Binya arrived, flushed and breathless, and went dashing into the stream after the umbrella.

Meanwhile, a tremendous fight was taking place. Locked in fierce combat, the two boys swayed together on a rock, tumbled on to the sand, rolled over and over the pebbled bank until they were again thrashing about in the shallows of the stream. The magpies, bulbuls and other birds were disturbed, and flew away with cries of alarm.

Covered with mud, gasping and spluttering, the boys groped for each other in the water. After five minutes of frenzied struggle, Bijju emerged victorious. Rajaram lay flat on his back on the sand, exhausted, while Bijju sat astride him, pinning him down with his arms and legs.

'Let me get up!' gasped Rajaram. 'Let me go—I don't want your useless umbrella!'

'Then why did you take it?' demanded Bijju. 'Come on—tell me why!'

'It was that skinflint Ram Bharosa,' said Rajaram. 'He told me to get it for him. He said if I didn't fetch it, I'd lose my job.'

6

By early October, the rains were coming to an end. The leeches disappeared. The ferns turned yellow, and the sunlight on the green hills was mellow and golden, like the limes on the small tree in front of Binya's home. Bijju's days were happy ones as he came home from school, munching on roasted corn. Binya's umbrella had turned a pale milky blue, and was patched in several places, but it was still the prettiest umbrella in the village, and she still carried it with her wherever she went.

The cold, cruel winter wasn't far off, but somehow October seems longer than other months, because it is a kind month: the grass is good to be upon, the breeze is warm and gentle and pine-scented. That October, everyone seemed contented—everyone, that is, except Ram Bharosa.

The old man had by now given up all hope of ever possessing Binya's umbrella. He wished he had never set eyes on it. Because of the umbrella, he had suffered the tortures of greed, the despair of loneliness. Because of the umbrella, people had stopped coming to his shop!

Ever since it had become known that Ram Bharosa had tried to have the umbrella stolen, the village people had turned against him. They stopped trusting the old man, instead of buying their soap and tea and matches from his shop, they preferred to walk an extra mile to the shops near the Tehri bus stand. Who would have dealings with a man who had sold his soul for an umbrella? The children taunted him, twisted his name around. From 'Ram the Trustworthy' he became 'Trusty Umbrella Thief'.

The old man sat alone in his empty shop, listening to the eternal hissing of his kettle and wondering if anyone would ever again step in for a glass of tea. Ram Bharosa had lost his own appetite, and ate and drank very little. There was no money coming in. He had his savings in a bank in Tehri, but it was a terrible thing to have to dip into them! To save money, he had dismissed the blundering Rajaram. So he was left without any company. The roof leaked and the wind got in through the corrugated tin sheets, but Ram Bharosa didn't care.

Bijju and Binya passed his shop almost every day. Bijju went by with a loud but tuneless whistle. He was one of the world's whistlers; cares rested lightly on his shoulders. But, strangely enough, Binya crept quietly past the shop, looking the other way, almost as though she was in some way responsible for the misery of Ram Bharosa.

She kept reasoning with herself, telling herself that the umbrella was her very own, and that she couldn't help it if others were jealous of it. But had she loved the umbrella too much? Had it mattered more to her than people mattered? She couldn't help feeling that, in a small way, she was the cause of the sad look on Ram Bharosa's face ('His face is a yard long,' said Bijju) and the ruinous condition of his shop. It was all due to his own greed, no doubt, but she didn't want him to feel too bad about what he'd done, because it made her feel bad about herself; and so she closed the umbrella whenever she came near the shop, opening it again only when she was out of sight.

One day towards the end of October, when she had ten paise in her pocket, she entered the shop and asked the old man for a toffee.

She was Ram Bharosa's first customer in almost two weeks.

He looked suspiciously at the girl. Had she come to taunt him, to flaunt the umbrella in his face? She had placed her coin on the counter. Perhaps it was a bad coin. Ram Bharosa picked it up and bit it; he held it up to the light; he rang it on the ground. It was a good coin. He gave Binya the toffee.

Binya had already left the shop when Ram Bharosa saw the closed umbrella lying on his counter. There it was, the blue umbrella he had always wanted, within his grasp at last! He had only to hide it at the back of his shop, and no one would know that he had it, no one could prove that Binya had left it behind.

He stretched out his trembling, bony hand, and took the umbrella by the handle. He pressed it open. He stood beneath it, in the dark shadows of his shop, where no sun or rain could ever touch it.

'But I'm never in the sun or in the rain,' he said aloud. 'Of what use is an umbrella to me?'

And he hurried outside and ran after Binya.

'Binya, Binya!' he shouted. 'Binya, you've left your umbrella behind!'

He wasn't used to running, but he caught up with her, held out the umbrella, saying, 'You forgot it—the umbrella!'

In that moment it belonged to both of them.

But Binya didn't take the umbrella. She shook her head and said, 'You keep it. I don't need it any more.'

'But it's such a pretty umbrella!' protested Ram Bharosa. 'It's the best umbrella in the village.'

'I know,' said Binya. 'But an umbrella isn't everything.'

And she left the old man holding the umbrella, and went tripping down the road, and there was nothing between her and the bright blue sky.

7

Well, now that Ram Bharosa has the blue umbrella—a gift from Binya, as he tells everyone—he is sometimes persuaded to go out into the sun or the rain, and as a result he looks much healthier. Sometimes he uses the umbrella to chase away pigs or goats. It is always left open outside the shop, and anyone who wants to borrow it may do so; and so in a way it has become everyone's umbrella. It is faded and patchy, but it is still the best umbrella in the village.

People are visiting Ram Bharosa's shop again. Whenever Bijju or Binya stop for a cup of tea, he gives them a little extra milk or sugar. They like their tea sweet and milky.

A few nights ago, a bear visited Ram Bharosa's shop. There had been snow on the higher ranges of the Himalayas, and the bear had been finding it difficult to obtain food; so it had come lower down, to see what it could pick up near the village. That night it scrambled on to the tin roof of Ram Bharosa's shop, and made off with a huge pumpkin which had been ripening on the roof. But in climbing off the roof, the bear had lost a claw.

Next morning Ram Bharosa found the claw just outside the door of his shop. He picked it up and put it in his pocket. A bear's claw was a lucky find.

A day later, when he went into the market town, he took the claw with him, and left it with a silversmith, giving the craftsman certain instructions.

The silversmith made a locket for the claw, then he gave it a thin silver chain. When Ram Bharosa came again, he paid the silversmith ten rupees for his work.

The days were growing shorter, and Binya had to be home a little earlier every evening. There was a hungry leopard at large, and she couldn't leave the cows out after dark.

She was hurrying past Ram Bharosa's shop when the old man called out to her.

'Binya, spare a minute! I want to show you something.'

Binya stepped into the shop.

'What do you think of it?' asked Ram Bharosa, showing her the silver pendant with the claw.

'It's so beautiful,' said Binya, just touching the claw and the silver chain.

'It's a bear's claw,' said Ram Bharosa. 'That's even luckier than a leopard's claw. Would you like to have it?'

'I have no money,' said Binya.

'That doesn't matter. You gave me the umbrella, I give you the claw! Come, let's see what it looks like on you.'

He placed the pendant on Binya, and indeed it looked very beautiful on her.

Ram Bharosa says he will never forget the smile she gave him when she left the shop.

She was halfway home when she realized she had left the cows behind.

'Neelu, Neelu!' she called. 'Oh, Gori!'

There was a faint tinkle of bells as the cows came slowly down the mountain path.

In the distance she could hear her mother and Bijju calling for her.

She began to sing. They heard her singing, and knew she was safe and near.

She walked home through the darkening glade, singing of the stars, and the trees stood still and listened to her, and the mountains were glad.

✗

Acknowledgements

Grateful acknowledgement is made to Penguin Books India for permission to use the following stories: 'All Creatures Great and Small', 'The Room of Many Colours', 'The Night Train at Deoli', 'The Woman on Platform No. 8' and 'Coming Home to Dehra'.

Printed in Great Britain
by Amazon

80312684R00124